sure
fire

MICHAELI TOM

Sure Fire

Trilogy Christian Publishers
A Wholly Owned Subsidiary of Trinity Broadcasting Network
2442 Michelle Drive, Tustin, CA 92780

Copyright © 2024 by Michaeli Tom

All Scripture quotations are taken from the ESV® Bible (The Holy Bible, English Standard Version®), copyright © 2001 by Crossway Bibles, a publishing ministry of Good News Publishers. Used by permission. All rights reserved.

All rights reserved, including the right to reproduce this book or portions thereof in any form whatsoever. For information, address Trilogy Christian Publishing Rights Department, 2442 Michelle Drive, Tustin, CA 92780.

Trilogy Christian Publishing/ TBN and colophon are trademarks of Trinity Broadcasting Network.

For information about special discounts for bulk purchases, please contact Trilogy Christian Publishing.

Trilogy Disclaimer: The views and content expressed in this book are those of the author and may not necessarily reflect the views and doctrine of Trilogy Christian Publishing or the Trinity Broadcasting Network.

10 9 8 7 6 5 4 3 2 1

Library of Congress Cataloging-in-Publication Data is available.

ISBN 979-8-89041-748-0
ISBN 979-8-89041-749-7 (ebook)

dedication

This book is dedicated to my three beautiful children, Beaux, Blair, and Brielle. The three of you keep me focused on what is important. Thank you for being so encouraging throughout this entire process. I pray that you always keep your eyes focused on the Lord so that He may guide your steps all the days of your lives.

Oh, the depth of the riches and wisdom and knowledge of God!

How unsearchable are his judgments and how inscrutable his ways!

—Romans 11:33

table of contents

Dedication iii

Prologue 9
Chapter 1: Beyond 13
Chapter 2: Confusion 21
Chapter 3: Alone 31
Chapter 4: Walk in the Woods 47
Chapter 5: Answers 59
Chapter 6: Glimpses 71
Chapter 7: Getting Closer 83
Chapter 8: First Date 97
Chapter 9: Truth Hurts 109
Chapter 10: Memory of a Goodbye 123
Chapter 11: Recognition 133
Chapter 12: Unexpected 143
Chapter 13: Hopeless 155
Chapter 14: One Way Home 169
Chapter 15: At Last 181

Author's Note 191
Scripture Glossary 193

vii

prologue

ichael was standing outside Elaine's open window, watching her world crumble around her... again. Elaine was lying on her bed, curled up in a tight ball and crying ever so softly. Michael ducked inside the window as quietly and quickly as he could. He sat in the blue antique reading chair Elaine had set in the corner of her small room between her large window and dark solid oak bookcase. The room's windows let in the beautiful autumn light and the wonderful scent of the pine trees surrounding her cozy mountain home.

If Michael were able to do anything at all to stop Elaine from falling apart, he would have done it in a heartbeat. He longed to hold her tight, stroke her hair, wipe away her tears, and tell her that everything would be all right. Yet, he was banned from any and all actual interference in Elaine's life. So, he sat there in the corner of her room, waiting for her to fall asleep. The least he could do was give her pleasant dreams due to her having to live in this nightmare.

The crisp autumn breeze was blowing the long, sheer white curtains ever so softly as if even nature was trying to ease Elaine's pain. The wind was caressing her cheeks and the nape of her neck and trying to dry the small stream of tears that had been flowing down her bruised face.

This was not the first time that Michael had seen Elaine like this, and it never took less of a toll on either of them. Her bottom lip was busted, she had a deep bruise across her left cheekbone, her neck had a handprint bruise wrapping around it, and her arms and legs were also covered in bruises in various stages of healing. She looked so frail and delicate lying there on her bed. Her long, wavy, dark red hair was flowing down over her pillow and splayed out over her bed.

There was nothing in Michael's world that was more precious to him than Elaine. He needed to protect her, and his inability to step in when she needed him most was breaking him. Knowing that Elaine would not be able to hear him, Michael began to speak. Her mind had begun to drift off to sleep, and this was all he could do to give her comfort. His voice was deep, soothing, and had an endearing hoarse quality to it that made it unique.

"Rest now, Elaine, and be at peace. I am here now, Elaine; feel my love and my presence. Let your mind and heart be at peace, for you are on the right path. Sleep now and know that I am here to give you strength."

Elaine gave a little stir, and Michael sat up quickly and silently. He didn't know what he was expecting, but it seemed as if she had actually heard him. Michael's heart leaped, and he began to repeat what he had been saying. That is when he saw a small smile spread across Elaine's hurt lips. She had heard him, and he was certain of that.

His heart had not been this full in a very long time. He sat in the quiet corner of her room all night. Watching Elaine sleep soundly, knowing that her dreams would give her hope and peace, Michael was captivated by every passing moment, and he wanted to be able to hold on to this for as long as he could.

For he knew that with the sunrise came pain. Pain that Elaine had to endure. Pain that Michael could not stop. All in an effort to finally break through and do what had never been done before. Hoping that Elaine might hear him again, Michael began to speak.

"I know that this is harder than anything you have had to endure before, but you have to hold on. Know that I am here with you always. I will never leave you, and you can pull strength from me when you need to. Always remember that I love you, and you are never alone."

Chapter 1

beyond

Everything began to fade away. Elaine was unable to see, feel, hear, or sense anything at all. She knows that she has passed on to the other side of life and is no longer tethered to her earthly body, feeling as if she has been trapped inside a great void. Suddenly, off in the distance, there seems to be a light shining. Elaine's body begins to drift closer and closer to this ever-growing radiant space. She feels like she is floating down a warm and peaceful river, being pulled ever so gently out of the darkness.

She is drifting faster and faster, ever closer to the light, until she is completely enveloped in its blinding white brilliance. Elaine remains floating in this warm, colorless place, being turned and twisted around as if she were being inspected by someone or, rather, something that she could not see. She is unable to move or do anything of her own volition. She comes to the realization that she is trapped like this and starts hoping for someone, something, or really anything to happen.

Suddenly, she feels a shock-like lightning coursing back and forth through her body. Every inch of her is being filled with a white-hot, searing pain. She desperately tried to scream out for help, but she was unable to make even a single sound. She is consumed with panic, and then she begins to fall.

She is falling faster and faster into the endless void beneath her. Her heart is racing at a rate she had never known before. In a state of pure terror, Elaine plummets further into the seemingly unending abyss below. Faster she falls, whirling, bending, unable to do a solitary thing about it. Her lungs are still unable to cry out for help, and then she brushes past something.

Again and again, things brush fiercely past, as if she is falling between the branches of two enormous trees. Unexpectedly, something has wrapped tightly around the upper part of her left arm. Whatever it is, it has latched itself onto her arm with incredible strength and instantly jerked Elaine out of her free fall.

Elaine's lifeless body is once again hanging suspended in the unknown space, but this time, the warmth and peace are far gone. They have been replaced by agony and fear. Something else wraps around her ankle, then her wrist, followed by her neck. That is when Elaine figured out what was restraining her: they were hands. Multiple hands that were pushing, pulling, and tearing at her helpless body. Squeezing ever so tightly, pulling in different directions with a force that has Elaine believing that she is about to burst open like a grotesque piñata. The sheer pressure from the holds on her body is enough to have her bones on the brink of shattering inside her helpless form.

She hears this scream echo into her mind, and at first, she thinks that she has finally gained some kind of control of this new body. But fear sets in when she notices that the scream is not coming from her. This voice is different, darker, and full of rage and hate.

"Well, well, well… Look what we have here," said the unfamiliar voice.

While the voice was almost enchanting in itself, and the words, harmless, Elaine couldn't help but feel power and anger radiating from the being that was now somewhere close to her immovable body.

"The precious Elaine. The perfect Elaine. How absolutely sick I am of having to hear about how wonderful you are."

Elaine was listening to this entrancing voice and trying to think of anyone who could come close to matching it. The more she tried to match it, the more she came up wanting. There is nothing as captivating and pure as this melodic yet completely terrifying voice that was rolling all over the place she was confined in.

"You used to just annoy me, my dear Elaine. This time, however, you seem to have crossed the line."

Hauntingly beautiful laughter sprung out from this mysterious entity and flowed so freely throughout the spaces in Elaine's mind.

"Now the sweet, precious Elaine has found herself here, alone and unprotected. How lucky am I?" the voice said mockingly.

Elaine was trying to move any part of her body, but it was as if she was encased in a tomb of flesh, unyielding and completely uncooperative to the wishes of its master.

"Now that I have you all to myself, where should I begin? Oh, I am just so excited to get… *No!*" the voice shouted in anger. "How did you get here?"

This terrifying wail continues to pierce Elaine's ears, shattering any train of thought that tries to piece itself together in her mind. All thought has gone as Elaine tries to figure out what is happening to her. She feels something cold and incredibly heavy being wrapped around her. Over and under, around and around, it was wrapped tightly around Elaine.

When the wrapping stopped, Elaine felt a new set of hands wrap around her shoulders. These hands are soft and gentle to the touch, contrasting harshly with the other hands currently grasping her wrist and ankle. A voice speaks gently into Elaine's ears at a volume in which even she is wondering if she heard anything at all.

"It is all right, I am with you now," the deep voice reassured her.

"What do you think you are doing?" boomed out from the man now holding Elaine's bound form. Elaine felt jostled and pulled in closer to the direction of the new voice.

"How dare you interfere with my work?" shrieked the terrifying voice, challenging this newcomer's very presence.

"How dare I? Are you serious? You know that no being is allowed to interfere with the crossing! This is so far beyond…"

"Oh, don't you dare try and lecture me! You know why I am here, and I will finish it this time!" The voice was becoming increasingly unpleasant. "I said, 'Let go of her'! You know she rightfully belongs to me! How dare you try to take her?" the now malicious voice shouts.

"I have been sent to retrieve this soul. You have no claim to her." This voice was deep and calm, like a peaceful river running through the countryside. Just hearing it put Elaine's whole body at rest.

"I will rip you apart! I swear you do not want to interfere with me this time, little brother. I shall have my revenge, and you will not be able to protect this disgusting, thieving vermin from my fury! She will suffer!"

Now, the calm voice was back in Elaine's ear, saying, "Get ready. We are about to be removed from this place. Can you control yourself yet?"

Elaine only stared ahead, still unable to focus her eyes, speak, or move. Her silence answered the question, and the voice began speaking in a language Elaine was sure she had never heard before. When he was finished, she was unleashed into her body.

"Yes, Father."

Elaine wondered what those two words meant and how they could possibly relate to the predicament that she was currently in. Not two seconds later, a shriek pierced through her; she tried to make out what the wicked beast had been shouting, but the end was lost in a whirlwind.

"You *cannot interfere!* You owe me this! I will finish this! I will find her, and I will kill…"

As the first voice faded out of Elaine's mind, her senses began to return to her body. Wind was whipping through her hair as she felt she was falling from a great height. For the first time in what felt like an eternity, Elaine was able to open her eyes.

She wasn't able to see anything through the tears in her eyes. She was unable to move due to whatever bound her body. She breathed in deeply the fresh air that she was flying through and let out the loudest cry for help that she could muster.

Before she was able to let out another scream, her lungs filled with something other than air. She had plunged into a freezing body of water. She continued to thrash around, trying to come out of her binds, but no matter how hard she tried to free herself, she continued to sink further below the water's surface.

Just as she was about to give up hope, a large hand gripped her bicep and began pulling her upward through the water's currents. As the two broke through the surface of the water, Elaine took a gasping breath and tried to cough up the water that she had inhaled.

The heavy bindings around her body began pulling her back into the frigid depths. Taking a deep breath before being submerged once again, Elaine began to fight her restraints. With the help of this mysterious being, she was able to free her arms and swim to the top.

"What in Sheol is going on?"

"Please, just calm down so I can help you."

"Who the heck are you?" she was able to squeak out of her throat between coughs.

"Stop!" the voice yelled. "I am trying to help you! Now, sit still. We only have a few days to get to the gates before she finds us, or this was all for nothing!"

"She who? Who in the depths of Sheol is she?"

"Would you just sit still? It's like I am trying to untangle a greased pig. All while trying not to drown myself."

"Who are you? Why are you helping me? And… why the hell am I in the middle of a freezing lake with a complete stranger? This makes absolutely no sense to me. I haven't done anything!"

"Why do you repeatedly bring that infernal place into our conversation? I can assure you it is no place that you would ever wish to find yourself."

The person swam in front of Elaine while mumbling to himself in that same language that sounded so foreign to her ears. He was now in her line of sight. Of all the things Elaine had pictured in her mind as to what this being looked like, it all fell flat. Never before had she seen such masculine perfection.

Bewildered by his appearance and response, Elaine stuttered out, "Oh… Okay… Well, you have yet to answer a single question I have asked you… Why are you helping me?"

He quietly chuckled to himself and then looked deep into her jade-green eyes and said, "I am helping you because you are my soulmate. I am helping you because I have searched for you since the dawn of time. I am helping you because you are finally here, and this is a big part of the purpose for my very existence."

If Elaine could have laughed without fear of drowning, she would have. This man must be the craziest person she has ever met.

"What the hel—"

The man flashed a warning glare toward Elaine, and she knew that she needed to rephrase her questions.

"What in the world are you talking about? You answered one question but created so many more that my head hurts! What do you mean by—Ouch!"

"Please, Elaine, just sit still. I have almost freed you from your bonds. Just wait, please."

With a few more pulls, Elaine was completely loosened from the ropes and chains that had been confining her movements. Now that she and her completely delusional companion were able to swim freely through the water, they headed to the north shore of the lake.

They swam together in total silence. The awkward atmosphere was only heightened by the long, arduous swim through the frigid waters. Swimming, floating, swimming, floating, on and on for as long as Elaine could push herself until, at last, she could stand.

Once the pair made it out of the water, Elaine collapsed on the sand. She was weary to her very core. Her muscles, tendons, and even her bones ached from the exertion she used to survive. In a matter of minutes, she had fallen into a deep sleep.

Dreams of the in-between place began to plague her restless mind. Memories of her body being pulled and fought over. The hauntingly beautiful voice echoing through her mind, ringing in her ears.

Chapter 2

confusion

E laine was shrouded in darkness, drifting down into an unfriendly abyss. Pain begins to radiate throughout her entire body. The shock of electricity pulsing through her veins as if it were blood. She tried to scream out for help, but her voice was not hers to command.

The pain stopped when she felt a hand wrap around her hair and begin dragging her off. Panic was the only emotion that filled her chest with dread. What had she done to deserve all of this? Why was this happening to her?

Suddenly, she was lifted and placed into a frosty metal chair. The startling shock to her nervous system made her wish for any type of mobility. Yet, she remained slouched and motionless in this new position, waiting for whatever came next.

"Did you think that I couldn't find you?" a terrifyingly beautiful voice called out to Elaine.

"Did you truly believe that I would give up that easily? Poor sweet Elaine. You have no idea what I am capable of!" the voice lazily hissed out, causing a shiver to snake its way down Elaine's spine.

Elaine couldn't believe that she had already been captured. She knew this hauntingly enchanting voice from the beyond and was utterly devastated. She tried to scream out once again, but unfortunately, once again, not a single sound escaped her lips.

"You are nothing more than a thief. Taking things that do not belong to you. And for what? Giving them over to him? You have done enough damage for all eternity! This time, you crossed the line!"

Elaine was equally as confused as she was terrified. A shiver ran down her spine and shook her to the very core. She had never stolen anything in her life. She was kind and honest and true. She had tried her best to be a light to those around her.

"You stay out of this, brother! No! Give her to me! She is rightfully mine, regardless of your feelings! She has stolen my..."

....

"WAKE UP!"

Elaine screamed as she was shaken awake. As her eyes sprung open, she was once again met by the most handsome face that she had ever seen. The deepest blue eyes were piercing through her very soul, calming her racing heart.

"You were screaming out in your sleep. I have been trying to wake you for a while now." His deep, raspy voice was able to bring her out of her panicked state.

"Thank you." That meek response was the only thing her mind could process while still reeling from that dream. Had she been found, or were her nerves finally getting the best of her?

"You're welcome," he said as he slowly stood up and walked to the other side of a fire that he must have built while she slept.

"Thank you for not letting me drown earlier too," Elaine painfully grunted as she struggled to sit up. She felt as if she had been hit by a truck. There was not a single muscle in her body that wasn't screaming out in pain. Every movement was pulling and burning as she twisted herself into an upright position. As she finally steadied herself in the sand, she let out an agonized breath.

Through the many noises and painful distractions of trying to move, if her companion even attempted to respond, she was unable to hear him.

Now that she was conscious and free to command her body's movements, she was able to study her companion. The warm glow of the firelight made his skin look as if it were made of bronze. His hair was blonde, and the mix of firelight and the various tones made it look as if it had been woven out of strands of pure gold. His oceanic eyes were framed by perfectly arched dark eyebrows and thick, long eyelashes. His cheekbones and jawline looked as if his face were carved to perfection out of the purest marble.

He had no blemishes. No fault in his impeccable appearance. On top of his immaculate appearance, he looked as if he could bench press a small car for fun. The muscle definition of this man was unreal. Yet, as she watched him staring into the fire, she was reminded of Atlas. It seemed as if the weight of the entire world was resting on his incredibly tense shoulders.

Sure Fire | Michaeli Tom

He was dressed in a charcoal grey T-shirt that snuggly hugged every rippling muscle of his arms and chest. He had black pants and big black boots that made him look as if he were on some sort of special ops mission. He also had a large tan bag sitting next to his feet. As Elaine gazed at him, she began to wonder where he had come from and why they were together in this completely unknown land.

As he sat next to the fire, his gaze still fixed on the flames, making him look almost predatory. Elaine felt as though she were watching a lion contemplate its next move. Calm and beautiful on the surface, but underneath, there was a wealth of power waiting to be released.

Elaine wanted to break the tension that had been building between the two. She knew nothing about her companion and decided to try to strike up a harmless conversation. All she had to comment on was what she had observed.

"So... are you some sort of bodybuilder or professional athlete?"

"No."

The one-word reply was all she was given in return. He didn't even lift his eyes from the flames to glance at her. She figured that he was lost deep in thought and that he didn't want to talk to her, or he truly was as crazy as she feared.

"Well, that was far more direct than any of your previous answers," Elaine said sarcastically.

She didn't know what she was trying to do at this point. She wanted to understand the person sitting across from her, at least until she could figure out what was happening to her.

Sure Fire | Michaeli Tom

"I don't even know your name. You seem to know my name for some unknown reason, but you haven't told me what your name is."

That seemed to do the trick. His head snapped up to meet Elaine's eyes, and when they did, she could see a flood of emotions threatening to break through.

"You truly don't know who I am?"

"I am sorry, but I have never met you before today."

He scoffed to himself as he looked back into the fire. The tension in his muscles was clear for her to see, as was the clenching and unclenching of his jaw in annoyance. Watching this stranger be so agitated should have unnerved Elaine, but all she could think about was figuring out who this person was supposed to be to her. He was so wound up, and she had to find the thread of conversation that would help her unwind the mystery of who they were to each other.

"How do you know who I am?" Elaine put as much emotion into her words as she could.

"I thought I answered that question while we were stuck in the lake. You and I are soulmates." His voice was every bit as masculine as his exterior, but the tone he used was soothing.

"You say that like it is supposed to mean something to me."

"Of course, it should mean something to you. It should mean a whole lot to you. It means that you are mine and that I am yours. I have fought to keep you safe over many lifetimes, and this past life was your last on earth. Now I finally get to bring you to the gates, and we can begin our lives there."

Sure Fire | Michaeli Tom 25

He sounded so genuine, almost relieved. Elaine couldn't figure out if what he said was more comforting or unnerving to her.

"Are you out of your mind? I have no idea who you are, why I am here, why you are 'helping' me... I mean, what are you helping me for? I thought once a person died, they went straight to heaven to be judged! I know I have died. I remember my life; well... pieces of it... maybe. All I know is I am now clearly not dead, but instead of being in heaven, I am met with a crash landing into an unknown land with a crazy person."

With a deep sigh, her companion looked up to the brilliant stars above them and began talking.

"Under normal circumstances, yes. You would have crossed the beyond and been deposited at the judgment seat. That is how it has worked for millennia now. Yet, these are anything but normal circumstances. I promise I will explain everything in time, but we must sleep. We have a four-day journey to the gates that will only open once on the sixth day; then, they will shut forever. On top of that, she could show up again at any moment. We will have to make better time than her and her army. Just, please, get some sleep."

Elaine's jaw was now on the floor. Her heart was about to beat out of her chest.

"How am I supposed to sleep now? Who is she? What could she possibly want with me?" Elaine was panicking, and then it dawned on her. "Ohhh no, is she the one from the beyond place? What did I do to her? And how did she get an entire army?" Frantically, Elaine was spouting off every question that was coming to her mind. Questions were flying faster and faster, mirroring her rapidly beating heart.

"I promise to tell you everything after you rest. You received your new body, but it is not invincible. You still require sleep, food, water, and protection. I can only help with keeping you safe and fed. You must rest now."

"New body?" She looked at her youthful hands, white gown, and healthy, deep red-colored hair that ran down her back and pooled in her lap. "You do know that every time you open your mouth, it raises about fifty new questions, right?"

He smiled a quick sideways grin at her before he started talking to himself under his breath. Then he reached into a tan nap sack that he had slung across his body. He pulled out a very old and delicate-looking flask.

"Here, drink some of this. It will help heal the scrapes and bruises you received while in the lake."

A loud bubble of laughter came out of Elaine's chest.

"I don't think so, buddy. I am A-OK."

A look of confusion crossed the man's face.

"Don't look at me like I'm the one that is crazy. You have been spouting nonsense this whole time and now want me to drink something. No, thank you."

"Suit yourself," he said with a cocky grin.

He pulled the cap from the top of the silver flask and began drinking whatever was inside. Elaine's mouth was suddenly as dry as cotton. She regretted her refusal of the drink, and so she cleared her throat to say, "It could have been poisoned or drugged. I didn't know if it was safe."

"No, you didn't trust me. Do you want some?"

Unwilling to verbalize her submission, Elaine nodded her head a single time. She took the container, relieved to have something to quench her thirst. She took a few large gulps of the delicious fluid and then returned the container to the handsome man trying to help her.

"Thank you."

"It… may… also help you sleep." Michael tried to mumble the last bit so she wouldn't hear him.

"Are you serious?" she asked dumbfounded. "Like now I feel better, so I can rest easy, or is this about to knock me out? Are you going to kill me? Is that what you are planning?"

"What? Have you listened to a single word I have said?" he said incredulously.

"Of course, I have. You have told me almost nothing of any real value."

Elaine's head began slowly spinning, and she could feel her eyes slipping closed. A peaceful weightlessness was spreading out and covering her body like a warm blanket.

"I saw you drink some of that too." She slurred the words out.

No matter how hard she was trying to stay awake, she was about to fail. In a last-ditch effort to find something out about this man, she said, "Can I at least know your name? I need to know something real about you!"

He grinned that same adorable grin at her weary form while he answered, "My name is Michael. You should remember me soon. Sleep now, my love."

Sleep she did. This time, she was not haunted by the woman from the beyond. This time, she was wrapped in this warm blanket of peaceful dreams. Dreams of a place she had no memory of, but it felt like home.

Chapter 3

alone

*E*laine was in the most beautiful mountain range she had ever seen. Tall snow-capped mountains with the largest pine trees growing freely up each incline. The dense pine forest was a perfect place for wildlife to live abundantly. Beautiful deer eating the plentiful clover fields. Chipmunks and squirrels scampered between the ancient trees while the birds of every color sat and sang the most enchanting songs.

Elaine was standing at the edge of the clearing, watching the animals wander through the forest. Stepping into the clearing, she turned to admire the magnitude of the landscape in which this settlement nestled into. Huge pine trees reaching up into the pure blue sky. Each tree made the Redwood Forest look meager and unimpressive. Elaine thought if she could climb to the top of one of the trees, surely she could touch a cloud.

Elaine twirled through the ancient forest, enjoying the cool breeze as it brushed across her cheek. She ran her hands across the beaded bodice of her dress. As she looked down, she saw that she was wearing an elegant black ball gown. She looked as if she were going to attend one of the Venician balls she had always wanted to go to.

Elaine turned her face back to the clearing, where she found a lovely log cabin. Small clouds of smoke were puffing out the top of a very large stone chimney on the back wall of the cabin. The floor-to-ceiling windows allowed her to see inside the home. It looked so cozy and wonderful. In the center of the living space sat a large russet sofa that was facing the enormous grey stone fireplace that was currently burning some wood that smelled like a sweet cedar. The comforting smell of the smoke filled her nose and warmed her heart.

"Elaine, where are you? Elaine..."

She could hear someone calling to her from the cabin. The voice was so familiar to her, but she couldn't see who it belonged to. She began focusing on trying to place that voice, but no matter how hard she tried, it slipped away. She was trying so hard to match a face to the voice calling out to her that she pulled herself from her dream.

Groggily, Elaine began to open her eyes. At first, she saw only a beautiful blue sky spotted with giant fluffy white clouds. She couldn't for the life of her remember where she was nor how she had ended up sleeping outside.

Then, all at once, everything from the past, however long, came crashing down upon her conscious mind. All of the horror and confusion from dying, the peaceful beyond, being taken, crashing into a freezing lake, and being stranded in the wilderness with a complete stranger.

Wait... the guy.

Michael.

Elaine sat up too quickly for her recovering body. Her head began pounding as she tried to look at her surroundings. The remnants of their shared campfire sat where it had been, but now only she remained. The space that had been occupied by her confusing companion was now abandoned.

Elaine jumped to her feet and tried searching the horizon for Michael. She looked to her right and saw the deep blue waters but no rescuer. In front of and behind Elaine were nothing but vast expanses of the sandy shores. A few logs and leafy debris were also scattered here and there upon the sand, but again, there was no sight of Michael.

To her left, Elaine saw a small grassy field that led to a great forest's tree line. Beyond the trees, Elaine could hardly see anything other than the rolling hills that served as their homes. While she was a bit scared of being all alone in the wilderness, she couldn't help but be in awe of the beauty that was surrounding her.

Never before had she seen nature in such a pristine state. The water was a brilliant blue that she could see all the way to the bottom. The shore was without a single piece of trash or broken glass. There was not a single thing out of place. That is with the exception of Elaine herself.

As she stood admiring the scenery, her stomach began to rumble. The hunger pains began to plague her entire being.

"Come on! Where am I even supposed to find anything edible?" Elaine began to wonder out loud.

She looked between the lake and the forest, trying to decide her best chance of happening upon food.

Sure Fire | Michaeli Tom

"I could try and catch a fish, but then I would have to cook it. I cannot build a fire, and the only person that I know who could have has vanished. I could traipse through the wild dark forest and hope that nothing finds and eats me. I might find a berry bush or a fruit tree in there, though… I could wait for Michael to come back. Please," she scoffs, "like he is coming back. Captain Crazy has left the building, and now I am here all on my own!" Elaine shouted into the wilderness, feeling conflicted.

On one hand, she was now alone and no longer had to entertain the mystery of her odd companion. On the other hand, she was alone. While the presence of Michael did unsettle her, at least nothing in its right mind would have dared to try and harm her while he was next to her.

After a few moments of deliberation, Elaine announced, "I choose not starving to death, but first, I need to rinse off. I guess I will take a dip in the lake. And now I am talking to myself; maybe I am the crazy one."

Elaine shook off the strange feeling and began walking to the lake to rinse off before her great adventure. As she neared the water, she remembered Michael's words about her "new body." She was nervous to see her reflection and see someone that she did not recognize.

As she finally reached the water's edge, she mustered up her courage and slowly peered down. She was greeted by a beautiful heart-shaped face. Large jade green eyes shone brightly under her dark red eyelashes. Upon closer inspection, she noticed the shining gold flecks that were scattered through her emerald irises. A smattering of light freckles covered her high cheekbones and thin nose. Her lips were plump and a light shade of pink that contrasted beautifully with her olive-toned skin. Her familiar red velvet-colored hair was flowing down her tall and curvy frame.

All in all, she felt as if she looked more like herself now than she ever had. She looked strong yet soft, beautiful yet fierce. She looked unstoppable. She felt empowered by being her true self.

She felt as if she looked like a warrior if that warrior wore a plain white cotton dress. It was simple and fell to her knees. It reminded her of something that would be worn in a hospital.

She knelt down in the sand and reached her right hand into the water. She began scrubbing off all of the sand and grime that had stuck to her body. She removed mud and ash and blood from her arms and legs, but to her surprise, she didn't have any cuts or bruises.

Once she was finished with her impromptu bath, she felt like a new woman. She felt refreshed and ready to go find something to make the rumbling in her stomach cease.

She took a few deep breaths as she began walking through the grassy field in an attempt to make herself brave enough to enter the dark woods that loomed up before her. The air smelled sweet, filled with pine and other earthy tones that could put anyone at ease. The more she tried to steady herself with her deep breaths, the better it worked. "Be strong and courageous" was the mantra that she kept telling herself over and over with each deep breath.

By the time she reached the enormous trees, she wasn't scared of anything that she might find. All was quiet, or what could be classified as eerily quiet, but Elaine found solace in the quiet. To her, quiet meant peace; quiet meant safety. Now, in the comforting silence, she began searching in the woods for any tree or bush that could yield any type of nourishment.

Elaine walked for hours humming different tunes to entertain herself, all the while looking everywhere she knew to find food. She had seen a few different types of mushrooms throughout her journey, but she had never learned which types were edible and which were poisonous. Knowing that most were not for consumption, Elaine decided to forego that roll of the dice and find something a little less dangerous.

She walked in relative silence through the dark wilderness for hours, the only noise coming from her and her outbursts of frustration. The sun was beginning to settle in among the trees, and Elaine was beginning to feel as if she had made a huge mistake. She had been entirely alone all day. She wasn't even able to see any type of wildlife, and she began to wonder if nature itself was avoiding her.

At last, Elaine saw a bush absolutely over-encumbered by the amount of orange berries it carried on its branches. They were round in shape and looked overly appetizing to Elaine's empty stomach. She began grabbing handfuls of the berries and eating them as quickly as she could. The berries tasted very similar to the cherry tomatoes that Elaine used to grow in her gardens.

After her fifth handful of berries, Elaine heard some leaves rustling behind her. She stood up quickly and turned and found herself face to face with an angry Michael.

"Tell me you did not just eat any of those berries!" Michael said while pointing to the bush Elaine had just raided for her snack.

"Why? They taste just like the tomatoes I used to grow. Would you like some?"

"Elaine, they are Jerusalem cherries! They are poisonous! Why didn't you wait for me!"

"I was starving, and I didn't see you anywhere! Why did you abandon me?"

"Abandon you? I knew you would be hungry when you woke, so I went to get you actual food! You were gone when I got back! Do you know how terrifying that was? I thought she got you!" Michael exploded and saw Elaine shrink a little into herself. "I'm sorry. I am not mad at you. I was scared that you were gone somewhere that I could not protect you."

"How did you find me then?" Elaine asked in a small voice.

"I have been searching for you and finding you for eons! Having a head start of a few hours in the woods wasn't that much of a challenge," Michael jested in an attempt to lighten the mood, "but it seems I wasn't quick enough." Michael sighed.

"What do you mean? Am I really going to die from eating these?" Elaine said desperately.

"No, you aren't going to die. You are going to be needing some of the things I brought, though."

Michael crouched and began digging through his tan bag once more. He pulled out containers and pouches and a new pair of shoes and clothes. He handed Elaine a container of a dark liquid that smelled of spices.

Sure Fire | Michaeli Tom

"Where did you get all of this stuff?" Elaine asked as she took inventory of the bag's contents.

"Our old cabin in the mountains to the west of the lake. It took me a while to get there and back, but I'm glad I went as soon as I did."

Michael took back the flask and set everything out in an order that suited him. Everything had its own place and purpose for being there.

"Our old cabin? What are you talking about?"

"The home that we were given to use between your assignments. All of the Sure Fires were gifted with a temporary home to recharge between assignments. I brought you some of your old clothes to change into. Here, put these on."

Michael handed the clothes and boots to Elaine as she sat dumbfounded. No matter how hard she tried to wrap her mind around the things Michael told her, she always felt as if she were living in someone else's story. How had things gotten so complicated?

"Hurry and get changed. We still have to get you taken care of, and the sun is about to set. I need to start a fire so that we have enough light to see by."

Elaine took the clothes and walked a short distance away to hide behind a tree. She quickly put the pants and boots on before she traded the gown for the long-sleeved black top. To her surprise, everything fit her perfectly. As she made her way back to Michael, she noticed that the fire had started, and the flames lit the surrounding area in a warm glow.

"Here, drink two big drinks of this," he said sternly.

Elaine knelt down and did as he asked, then she returned the container to him. She sat in silence for a while as he continued grabbing different parcels and organizing them to his liking.

He took the white gown from Elaine's hands and threw it into the fire. "We don't need this anymore, and we can't leave it here for them to find or track us by."

"I guess that makes sense..."

"You are about to vomit," Michael said calmly.

"What do you mean by that?" Elaine questioned. Before Michael was able to respond, she jumped up from her seated position and ran to the nearest tree to have support as she rid her stomach of all of its contents.

Michael walked up behind her and held back her long locks. He rubbed soothing circles on her back as he tried to help her in any way he could.

Once she had finished and stood up again, she shot a glare at Michael. "Why did you do that to me?" she inquired in a very accusatory tone.

"You ate something poisonous and needed to get it out of your system before it did any further damage. Now here, take this."

"Yeah, right! The last two drinks you have given me haven't ended in anything pleasant."

"Elaine, I am not playing with you. I need you to trust me because I am the only thing keeping you alive right now!" Michael sighed and took a deep breath and then said, "Look, I know you don't remember me yet, but you will. I would never do something that would hurt you! That I swear to you."

Sure Fire | Michaeli Tom

"And last night, you knocked me out."

"Last night, I gave you a medicine that was supposed to rejuvenate your body. You were so depleted that you had to sleep for the medication to work. I didn't realize how injured you had been, and for that, I apologize."

"I'm supposed to thank you for that, I guess... I did wake up with no bruises, and my muscles don't hurt all that much."

"Will you at least rinse your mouth with the water?" Michael asked with his left eyebrow quirked slightly.

"Yes, thank you," Elaine said as she took the canister from Michael.

The cool water swished around her mouth before she spat it on the ground. She took a few more gulps of the refreshing liquid before she returned the canister to Michael. When she handed the water to Michael, his warm, rough fingertips brushed hers as his eyes bore into her soul. Emotions she had always wished to see in her husband's eyes were coming through the eyes of a total stranger. It made Elaine shudder a little as she remained locked into Michael's gaze.

"You need to eat something, but if your stomach begins to hurt, tell me immediately. You will need to take another dose of your favorite medicine." Michael chuckled to himself.

"I will eat, but I can tell you already that I am not feeling well," Elaine said with a grimace.

Michael nodded and took a deep breath. "Well, the sooner you drink it, the sooner you will start feeling better. Food first, though," he said over his shoulder as he grabbed a box filled with nuts, small dried fruits, and fresh berries of every color.

Elaine ate as much as she was able before her stomach began cramping too painfully. She looked at Michael before she drank from the medication flask once again.

"You will be here when I wake up, won't you?"

Michael chuckled loudly as she began drinking her medication. Elaine gave him a disapproving look as she capped the flask once more.

"If I have learned anything, it is that I cannot leave you unattended for any length of time," Michael teased.

By the look on Elaine's face, the joke was not appreciated.

"I will not leave your side, even for a moment. I promise you. I will watch over you as you recover."

The honesty and determination that Elaine saw burning in the depths of Michael's eyes told her that he was being truthful. She could feel herself beginning to trust this stranger, and she felt a certain peace around him that she found nowhere else.

"Is there any way that you could tell me a story as I try to fall asleep? Just something to distract me from this burning in my stomach. It feels as if I'm being stabbed," Elaine said through grunts of pain.

"I'm not known for my storytelling abilities."

"I just need something to keep my mind occupied. Please?" Elaine said in an almost desperate manner.

As Michael watched her clutching her stomach, he reluctantly replied, "I will give it my best shot."

It took him a few moments to think of a story to tell her. She no longer knew who he was. She couldn't even remember who she was herself. The chiasm between the two seemed so vast, and Michael was at a loss for where to even begin. After a moment of contemplation, he began to speak in a somber, low tone.

"A very long time ago, when the world had taken its shape and began to support the life of all the creatures that the Creator was placing upon its surface, the moon and the stars filled the night sky, and the sun illuminated the day for all creation to follow its path. Angels loved watching Him make all of these immensely different beings out of nothing at all and wondering how He could continue to make these intricate living beings so unique and different from one another." His deep voice rumbled through the night air. It was almost as if his voice was a tender caress that eased the ache in Elaine's body, and she was finding herself slowly being able to relax.

"That sounds lovely. This is going to be a good story, I can tell," Elaine said with a small smile tugging at her lips.

"It was fantastic. He orchestrated everything so precisely, so perfectly, that the harmony of the creation would simply sing as it existed. Then, one day, as they were watching Him, He began forming something out of the dirt. He worked on it for such a long time. Once He was satisfied with His work, He breathed life into the being. It was incredible. It was made in His likeness and had the same ability to create wonders out of almost nothing at all. The only downfall was that they were so easily distracted, and that was a weakness that could easily be exploited."

Elaine yawned deeply and then asked, "So, what happened next?" Her voice was incredibly soft and breathy due to the medicine kicking in.

"The Creator is perfect in all of His ways. He lacks nothing and gives everything that is good and pure to His creation. He is all that is kind, good, light, forgiving, loving, and wonderful, and He knew that He would have to step in and offer a way to deliver His creation from their sins if He bestowed them with free will. He knew they would have to know the darkness outside of His presence to understand the depth of His light and love. He also knew that they would forever be plagued by the enemy through their lies and deceptions. While people had a cosmically engrained need to connect to Yahweh woven into their very being, the evil that was unleashed into the world created such confusion and devastation that the humans couldn't even recognize what it was that they were missing in the first place." Michael stopped to look over at Elaine to check if she was asleep yet.

"I am still up. I'm just resting my eyes," Elaine mumbled and then proceeded to yawn loudly.

"If you say so." Michael chuckled. "Anyway, Yahweh planned to send out anchors for the humans to lean on in their time of need. He called them Sure Fires because they were created to have their souls burn so bright that every person who crossed their path would catch fire for the Lord just by being in their presence. The Sure Fires were designed to go into the world as pairs, but Lucifer rose up her army before they could be sent out. All the Sure Fire pairs that had been bound to a fallen angel turned into Dark Fires. Their wicked counterpart wreaked havoc on their souls and used their bonds to commit atrocities against the humans. As brightly as they shone before they fell was equal to the depth of darkness that they now unleashed upon the face of the world. None were so vile as the cursed one." The deep tones of Michael's voice seemed to turn even darker as he recalled the events.

He turned to check on Elaine once more and found her sound asleep. The soft glow of the firelight made her dark red hair look as if it were fire itself. The small, comfortable smile that was on her face as she slept reassured Michael of his efforts. He wasn't sure how much of the story Elaine would remember, but he could see that the effort he had put into taking care of Elaine was finally beginning to wear down some of her thick walls. He was determined to break down each and every one until she fully trusted him once more. Her peaceful smile filled him with hope for their future.

"Please, remember me! I know this is hard right now, but if you could just remember who we were in the past, this would be so much easier. I will always do everything in my power to protect you from any and all harm. I would fight the devil and all the armies of darkness to keep you out of harm's way, but I need you. We were created to be a team. Just please, please try and remember who you are supposed to be." Michael said these words with a heavy heart. His heart sat not five feet from him, but she was just as unreachable as she was when she was sent to the mortal realms. He felt as if everything they had gone through was in vain. Lucifer had managed to ruin something else with her need for vengeance.

"Father, I am in desperate need of guidance. I don't know where I am supposed to go from here. Please, guide my steps and lead me in the way I am meant to go. I ask that you keep us protected from every form of darkness that would try to do us harm. If it is your will, allow us to make it safely to the gates and not be overtaken. I am grateful for this opportunity to serve; I just ask to be successful in carrying out your commands." Once Michael finished his prayer, he closed his eyes and tried to get some rest.

Chapter 4

walk in the woods

As Elaine awoke, she found herself looking up at Michael's face as he carried her through a dense forest. There were many different types of trees surrounding them as they walked through the small valley, making each tree look ancient and vast. The canopy of leaves above them was almost enough to completely block out the afternoon sun. The light that made it through the leaves and branches formed a delicate lace pattern across Elaine's face.

She could feel the tight muscles of his arms and chest as he cradled her. Michael might still be a stranger to Elaine, but she had never felt so protected and safe in her life. Somehow, being this close to Michael made her feel like she was finally home. She was completely at rest there in his arms.

"I have felt you around me. I mean, before, in my life, I have felt your presence even though I couldn't see you. Haven't I?"

Michael stopped walking and held Elaine a bit tighter when he answered, "I had hoped that you were able to."

"That's it? For someone that is supposed to be my soulmate, you give me almost nothing to go off to get to know you."

Michael gently set her on her feet before he took her hands in his. Sadness covered his face as he looked down into her eyes.

"Angels aren't supposed to meddle in the lives of mortals. We are to be the small voice in the back of your mind, lending you guidance and advice. Actual interference in the mortal realm is only allowed in dire circumstances. Even if the particular mortal you are trying to help is your soulmate."

"Angels?"

"Yes."

"Are you trying to say that you are an angel?"

"Yes," he answered in the same unwaveringly confident tone.

"Aren't you supposed to play the harp or float on a cloud wearing a diaper? You look a little too aggressive to be an angel."

"Are you being serious right now?" Michael looked completely offended at her depiction of angels. "Of course, we don't look like babies in diapers. We are warriors. We were meant to be protectors. We have been sent out into the world to be guardians of our soul-bonds."

"All biblical mention of you guys said you were these terrifying beings casting fear into anyone that you met. Why am I not scared of you then?"

"You are not afraid of me in part due to being soul-bound to me. Also, you have received your celestial body. You see me as I am meant to be seen, not with mortal eyes."

48   *Sure Fire* | Michaeli Tom

Michael could see the questions bubbling up inside of Elaine and chose to begin speaking again before the flood of questions began flowing down upon him.

"You see, once our soulmate has been sent to live out their life, or lives, in your case, on earth, we must then go and find them to serve as their guardian. We do not know where or even when you will be sent to live, and therefore, we must search to find and protect you. Every life you were sent to live, I found you. Every time, I would end up getting too close. I hated seeing you frightened, hurt, sad, or broken-hearted over someone who didn't deserve the type of love that you showed to everyone around you. So, when you would go to sleep, I would come to you and give you peaceful dreams. I tried to help you rest, even if only for a short while."

Elaine was dumbstruck. Words were now stuck in her throat. Looking up at this man, she only saw hurt and despair in his azure orbs.

"Why would you not know where I was?"

"We were supposed to be paired, but after the fall... so many fell from grace. There were so many humans that no longer had their guardians. So many that were left unprotected and deceived. We were then sent blindly into the world so that whoever we came across, we would help. We had to stand in the gap that was created by others' selfishness."

"That story from last night... was that real?" Elaine said in an unsure tone, her head tilted to the side in disbelief as she tried to fit the pieces together.

Sure Fire | Michaeli Tom

"That story was the beginning of everything. The start of our existence and our purpose. I hoped that if you heard that story, it may awaken something that has been locked away."

"I guess it didn't work because I don't even remember how you ended the story. I thought you were making up a bedtime story, so I didn't pay attention." Elaine sighed in annoyance.

Michael lowered his eyes and paused. The hurt that was packed into his voice caused Elaine's heart to clench painfully in her chest. Seeing this seemingly unbreakable being come undone was unnerving. She didn't know how to help him get through this hurt.

"Did I not do a good job? I did try my very best."

"What do you mean?"

"I mean that I did everything that I could. I could not physically step in and do anything to those around you, or I would have. I tried to keep you out of harm's way as often as the rules would allow. I sent warnings, created diversions, and amplified the feelings given to you through your intuition, but I could not do much in the means of physically removing you or the people around you. I wanted to, believe me. I had to be restrained a few times by my brothers this past life, but I couldn't do more."

"Because you are an angel?"

"Yes."

"What exactly do you mean by yes?"

"Exactly that."

"Would you care to explain how my soulmate is an angel and not another, I don't know, human? You know, like me?"

50   *Sure Fire* | Michaeli Tom

Elaine was overwhelmed in every sense of the word. Every time she had a conversation with Michael, it felt as if she were being left further and further behind. At this rate, Elaine felt as if she were never going to catch up to what was truly going on.

"Human? You are a Sure Fire, and none of you has a human as their soulmate," was the exasperated reply that Elaine received. Michael looked confused for a while as he searched Elaine's eyes for any sign of recognition. After a few moments, he pulled back, and then he said, "You truly don't remember anything other than this life, do you?"

"No… Am I supposed to? And what do you mean by Sure Fire?"

"Damn you, Lucy! She didn't succeed in stealing or killing your soul, but she was able to disrupt the restoration process enough to keep you from regaining your memories. I thought they would have returned to you as you slept, but I see they haven't… How many lives do you remember?"

"My one and only," was the sarcastic reply that Elaine gave to Michael.

"She made sure that you only remembered strife and turmoil. You don't even remember me, well, anything other than the essence of me. That must be why He sent us here as a head start."

"Umm, excuse me. You have said *she* since I got here, which I assume is your pal Lucy? Now, there is a He? Both of which I am completely out of the loop as to who they are and what they could possibly want with me!"

"Yes, you do. You are just unable to remember that you do know." Michael huffed.

"What is that supposed to mean? How am I supposed to remember before I... was? I'm not even sure how to word that properly," Elaine said exasperatedly.

"For it is written in Jeremiah 1:5, 'Before I formed you in the womb I knew you.' The Creator was talking to Jeremiah, telling him of the intimate relationship that they had before he was put on the earth. All the heavenly hosts knew you, and you knew us. The fall ripped through us all and caused such a division," Michael said with sadness in his deep voice.

"Michael, I am feeling so miserably behind on everything. Can you please, just this once, answer me in something other than riddles? I am starting to feel as though you are purposefully keeping me in the dark."

"The Creator, of course, is the Creator of existence, Yahweh. He helped us because of our unending faithfulness and devotion. Naturally, she is trying to disrupt His plans for her own selfish desires once again."

Michael spat the word "she" as if it were poison. Elaine could feel the seriousness of his words and could sense something awful coming. She didn't want to push Michael too hard for fear of him shutting her out once again. All she could manage to say was, "Lucy?"

"Lucifer." Spat Michael once again.

This was the absolute last thing Elaine was expecting to hear him say.

"Lucifer," she repeated, shocked. "Hold on a dang second! Why is Lucifer wanting to destroy my soul? Also, since when has Lucifer been a woman?"

"She has always been female. She was the most beautiful, most talented, most trusted, and most beloved of all the angels. When she spoke, she had a way of making everyone around her listen. She composed herself in a way that demanded respect, if not total devotion. When she sang, the Creator Himself turned to listen to the perfection that came from her lips."

"You speak of her as if you loved her."

"Everyone loved her. When she fell... it was hard on everyone." The sadness and betrayal Michal felt were clearly on display before Elaine for a brief moment. Then he composed himself and hid his emotions so well it was hard for Elaine to tell if he even had any at all.

Michael turned to begin walking down the path he and Elaine were traveling down. His nonchalance about everything that he had just said was making Elaine feel insane. How could this be her reality? How has her simple life turned into a complete rollercoaster of cosmic proportions?

"All right... she was wonderful until she wasn't." Jealousy tinged Elaine's voice, and she wasn't entirely sure why. She decided to change the subject quickly before Michael noticed her tone as well. "Why is she after me? I am a nobody."

"Be quiet!" Michael whispered in a worried tone.

"Are you kidding me? You said you would answer my questions!" Elaine shouted.

Michael wrapped his right arm around Elaine's waist and placed his left hand over her mouth. After a few seconds of silence had passed, Michael whispered, "I need you to be very quiet! I need to be able to listen!" The desperation that was laced through his voice sent Elaine into high alert.

Elaine began to look around, unable to hear anything other than the wind in the trees. To her, everything was peaceful and calm. She couldn't pick up on anything being out of the ordinary, but when she looked at Michael, she could see the tension in his posture. She could see the storm brewing in his eyes. The once peaceful ocean of blue was now looking more like a hurricane that was gaining power to make landfall. When he looked at her again, the intensity of his gaze made her shiver.

Whatever he was hearing, she suspected it was not good news for her. The few tense moments of silence felt like an eternity for Elaine waiting to be clued in on what was happening again. She had never felt so out of her element.

"Hell hounds. They aren't close enough to catch our scent yet, but if we remain out in the open like this, we will be found."

"You are so full of crap! *Hell hounds?* Are you serious? You actually scared me, you jerk!" Elaine shouted as she shoved Michael's chest.

"I am being serious! If they catch our scent, they will lead her directly to us!"

"You expect me to believe that?"

"Yes, I do. Lucifer took the Creator's most loyal creation and completely mutilated it. Twisted and molded them into dark, decrepit spies for her to use as she pleases. Right now, every one of them is looking for you and me! We need to move. Now!"

Elaine scoffed at Michael's panic.

"And go where, genius? I don't even know where here is! Where do you expect us to hide?"

"We are in purgatory. It is a neutral place. Not on earth, but neither is it in the heavenly realms. There is a safe place about five miles from here, and we must make it there before the sun sets, or the door will be lost to us for the night. If we stay out here, the hounds will most definitely find us, and soon," Michael said as he took quick strides down the path.

"All right, how long do we have until sunset?"

"About two hours."

"Two hours? To make it five miles through the hills and wilderness. Not to mention that we have to find a hidden place before the 'magical' door vanishes. How long was I out if it is almost sunset?" Elaine shouted as she struggled to keep pace with Michael's long strides.

"You slept for almost a full day! Being here, that is about thirty-two human hours, give or take. I have carried you for around twenty-five hours, and now that you are capable of carrying yourself, I suggest that we run," Michael said in a tone that left no room for argument.

Elaine's thoughts were already running wild with all the new information that was always finding a way to penetrate her mind. This was all just too much. Too many things were working against her for reasons she didn't know or couldn't remember. Every time she thought she was making progress in learning about where she was or even who she was, she would be flooded with even more questions.

Now, Michael was pulling her behind him at an inhumane rate of speed. They were racing through the trees, dodging branches, and leaping over root clusters on the ground. For being such a large man, Michael was especially light on his feet. They were able to glide out of the shelter of the trees and into a field of grasses and wildflowers. Some of which Elaine had never seen before.

New turquoise, magenta, silver, black, and violet flowers grew wild in the field. All of the different sizes and shapes and scents enchanted Elaine as she ran along. The floral perfume that was filling the air was powerful yet completely addicting. It was pure and lovely. Elaine felt like she could live there in that field.

"These black, star-shaped flowers are incredibly potent and have a drug-like effect on the hounds. If we are lucky, it will mask our scent enough for them to be unable to track us. Here, rub these all over your body, but be quick."

Elaine should have been comforted by this news, but the strong aroma was beginning to make her head spin. She was having a hard enough time catching her breath without the added task and overpowering smells. She had been running for her life with a perfect stranger in an unknown land. She had a feeling that running from hell hounds left little time for her to stop and smell the roses, as it were. Yet, she did as Michael asked and rubbed the flowers all over her clothes and hair.

Once they were both coated in the flowers' scent, Michael and Elaine were back in their race against time. Elaine was running as hard as she could, trailing after Michael as he found their route to this hidden place. It had been years since her legs could carry her like this, but still, she was falling behind her guide.

They managed to leave the field of flowers behind as they entered a new dense forest. With the waning sun, the darkening trees looked like an ominous warning. A small voice in the back of her mind was telling her that she would never make it, that the darkness would swallow up her only chance of survival.

In defiance, she doubled down on her efforts and willed her body to keep going. She pushed her legs to run faster and tried to ignore the burning in her chest. She was never again going to fall subject to that little voice that ruled over her mortal life.

She looked up to find Michael taking a path slightly to her right that followed the bend around the base of a foothill. A small unused trail that would be almost invisible unless you knew where to look for it. The sun was setting, and every passing moment felt like another nail in Elaine's coffin. Panic was rising in Elaine's tightening chest. The pressure from everything felt as if it were compressing her heart and burning her lungs.

Then, Michael took an abrupt right turn and suddenly stopped. He was looking left and right as if he were unsure of his next move. Then clarity seemed to have struck him like a lightning bolt, and he started running hard, straight ahead once more.

"It is this way! We are close, but need to hurry," Michael shouted as he ran through the wilderness.

The sky was a deep red, with the sun almost out of sight, when Elaine heard Michael shout.

"Over here!"

Chapter 5

answers

*M*ichael grabbed a low-hanging branch from a large willow tree and pulled it down. The ground began to rumble, and a door inside the willow that Elaine had previously not seen began to open to an ancient staircase descending into darkness.

Michael motioned for Elaine to enter the passage, and without much hesitation, she did. Elaine's trust in Michael had continued to grow despite knowing so little about him. That fact frightened her. The people she trusted the most in her mortal life were the ones to hurt her the most.

Once they were both inside the shadowy tunnel, Michael turned to the small cutout in the wall and whispered something Elaine couldn't understand. A small light began to illuminate the dim space enough for Elaine to see. Beautifully carved marble stairs with walls carved in intricate designs that must have taken a very long time to complete. Symbols in sequence made Elaine believe that it was more a language than a design covering the most dazzling staircase she had ever seen. Long, wispy letters swirled around one another, looping in sequences that she was unable to decipher.

Someone must have worked very hard to make something this grand and beautiful, but everywhere Elaine looked, there was a thin layer of dust. This led her to believe that no one had been here in a very long time. Despite the very obvious absence of visitors, the air in the underground staircase smelled fresh and almost sweet.

Michael said something else in that enchanting foreign language, and the door sealed them inside.

"Come on, down we go."

"That language you just spoke. Is that the language that is on the walls?"

"Yes. It is the language of the Creator. These writings detail the history of our kind and all the wondrous events that happened here in purgatory. This place used to be well-traveled. Purgatory was a kind of staging area for the Creator while He was designing all living things. Everything that was to be placed on the earth was first thought up here. Watching Him bring to life all the incredible new creations was a wondrous sight to behold. All the hosts of heaven loved to bear witness to his works."

"Those flowers and trees in the fields. I have never seen those before. Did He not like them?"

"Of course, he liked them," Michael said with a half chuckle.

From this view, Elaine could see that his left lateral incisor was just a little crooked, making his otherwise perfect smile that much more endearing to her. She wasn't quite sure why this person was having such an impact on her, but every time she thought of him, she felt a little more at ease.

"He decided that some things were more suited for earth, while others should stay here or in heaven. He believed the same to be true with a few of the animals and sea creatures as well."

"What, like unicorns?" Elaine said sarcastically with a small chuckle.

"Yes."

The light from the solitary lamp at the top of the stairs was beginning to fade. Darkness was enveloping the pair as they began walking down into the mysterious depths of this place. Unable to see Michael's facial features clearly, Elaine could not tell if he was kidding with her or not.

"I'm not sure if you are being honest right now," Elaine said with a slight crinkle of her eyebrows.

The fading lights caused Michael to be almost totally encased in darkness, but Elaine could sense him smirking at her.

"I am. Only, unicorns also have wings. Somehow, every once in a while, a soul will be born, retaining a few of their celestial memories while living on earth. My guess is that the men and women who wrote about these creatures were only able to remember slivers of them. While recording them, they separated the unicorn into two species. A unicorn, or a magical horse with a horn on its head, and the pegasus, a flying horse. When in all reality, they are but one creature."

Sure Fire | Michaeli Tom

"How did they retain their memories? I can't even remember things that I am supposed to," Elaine said, a little frustrated with her circumstance.

"I am not sure. I believe that the Creator has a plan, but His ways are His own. I simply trust that He has everything worked out in His time, and I try to help in any way I can."

"Huh… So, are they still here? Can we find one here in purgatory?" Elaine said with the enthusiasm of a child.

"No. They have all been moved through the gates. Just about everything with a soul has already been removed from this place. You know, this would go much faster if you actually walked down the steps."

"Sorry," Elaine mumbled. "This is just blowing my mind right now. For instance, this place is beautiful. I mean, yes, it is also the place we have been dumped in to hide from the Mistress of Darkness herself, but… You said this is where everyone came to watch creation happen."

"It is beautiful, but…"

Elaine tripped and jerked Michael's arm in an attempt to regain her balance. There was no longer any light to see by, making Elaine hold on to Michael and the wall while slowly making their descent. She was putting her faith in Michael in the hopes that he knew what was down in this chiasm.

"Stand right here. One moment, it should be right about… here."

Elaine could hear the shuffle of Michael's feet as he tried to find some new mysterious object.

"Here it is," Michael said triumphantly.

He began whispering in the celestial language that Elaine began to love. She couldn't understand the words, but the feeling of comfort she received every time she heard it could not be replaced.

When he stopped speaking, the room was bathed in a fresh new light. It was a fairly large room with tall ceilings, beautiful dark wooden floors, and the same marble formed the walls as the staircase. In the far corner of the room stood a marble island with three large crystal vases. Each vase was filled with its own light.

"What do you keep saying to yourself?" Elaine asked.

"I don't keep saying anything to myself," Michael answered hesitantly.

"Yes, you do. Firstly, when we were at the top of the stairs, and then again just now. You weren't talking to me, and there is no one else here that could have heard you. So, you are either talking to yourself or to someone I am not seeing. And you only do it in the language of the Creator," Elaine said, indignantly.

"That is because it is the language of the heavens. I was speaking to the lights and earlier to the door, as you have pointed out. Celestial lights must be called by name before they will illuminate."

"God knows the stars, and He calls them by name," Elaine said softly, remembering Scripture. "What is this one's name?" She said, pointing to the first jar on the marble island.

"These are celestial lights, not stars. This one is Seraphina, and the blue one in the middle is Sashiel," Michael said with a fond smile on his face. Each time their names were spoken,

Sure Fire | Michaeli Tom

they shone just a little bit brighter, as if they were proud of being called upon.

"And the one on the end?" Elaine asked, perplexed as to why this one was left out.

"This one is special. Its name is Raguel. It keeps the harmony between the three."

"What is the difference between celestial lights and stars?"

"Celestial lights are simply that. Lights that we use to illuminate the dark spaces. Stars were created as footholds for us as a place where we could keep watch over creation, our sentry posts, if you will. A place in which we could bask in the glory of our Creator while being sent to the earthly realms for our different assignments. We are the stars that the Creator calls by name."

"So... in the Bible, when it is talking about stars, it is actually talking about angels?"

"Most of the time, yes. The same can be said about the mention of different trees being people. God loves imagery and parables that must be interpreted through the aide of the Holy Spirit. Otherwise, people would hardly seek Him to find the answers to their questions and problems."

"You are kidding, right?" Elaine paused to watch his face for any type of humor, yet found none. "You're being serious? You know, now that I think about it, Plato believed that every soul had a companion star. That once someone died, their soul would then ascend to its paired star, and together they would reside in the heavens forever."

"That would have been one of his celestial memories trying to point him back to the Creator."

"Is that why his beliefs are so close to that of Christianity? He lived such a long time before Christ came to earth, and yet his beliefs follow closely to His teachings."

"I cannot be certain. As I have said, the Creator works in His own time and in His own ways. All I know is that everything always works out if given enough time. Plato also had a very hard-working guardian; her name is Lailah," Michael said with a small smile.

Elaine walked closer to the island that came up slightly higher than her waist. She was admiring the depictions of creation that were carved into this structure. Instead of words and symbols, this had beautifully carved scenes.

The carving that most captivated Elaine's attention was that of one creature that was being split into two equal but whole parts. The looks on their faces showed no pain but instead a loving admiration. Elaine was marveling at the carvings while Michael was digging into the drawers at the end of the counter.

"What is this?" Elaine asked as she ran her fingers over the design.

"That is the creation of the soulmates. Where two came from one, kind of like when Eve was created out of Adam's rib."

"I remember a story like this from the Greek mythologies. The gods were jealous of the humans, so they split them into two parts, forever searching for the other half of themselves. I always thought it was strange."

"The best lies are the ones that are based on truths. Teaching humans that the gift of a soulmate was instead an act of

Sure Fire | Michaeli Tom 65

a group of jealous gods not only misguides them but instills a distrust between them and the true God."

"Is that why so many of the religions have the same basic stories and gods? They took the true story of creation and twisted it to fit their wants? Who could even do that?" Elaine asked.

"The fallen angels that were determined to do anything they could to ruin the connection between the Creator and His people. They set themselves up as gods to be worshiped in the place of the true Creator. They made him out to be a monster, and those of us who follow him were just as wicked."

"Are you portrayed as a god?" Elaine said in disbelief.

"Unfortunately, yes. I have been named Ares, Tyr, Skanda, Hachiman, and Mars, among others. Being the leader of the Creator's army, they have turned me into this bloodthirsty god of war. I have only ever fought for what was right and just: to protect those from the forces of the wicked. Yet, the fallen see me as a monster and have led most of mankind to share their sentiments."

Elaine's stomach growled loudly throughout the room. Instantly, her cheeks were tinged red with her embarrassment.

"We can finish our conversation about this after we get you fed. Let's see what we can find in here."

He started placing small wooden boxes on the counter close to Elaine. Once they had all been set out, he began opening them up one at a time. The boxes filled the room with an irresistibly delicious aroma. The smell alone had Elaine's stomach rumbling with hunger.

"Look what I have found," Michael called to her once he was finished unboxing all the supplies.

"I have some grapes, nuts, challah, and apricot preserves for dinner. You see, this used to be the basement of our resting place. It was used as a storage room for food, supplies, and other things we may require. Luckily, I have found a few boxes filled with enough food for us to eat for the next three days," Michael said with a smile on his face.

"Are you sure these things are still edible? Surely everything down here has gone bad by now," Elaine said with one brow slightly raised, showing her distrust of the offered foods.

"Decay and death are only part of the mortal realm. Here, everything remains untouched by their corruption," Michael said with a genuine smile on his lips.

"Okay... You said this used to be your resting place?" Elaine inquired as she hopped up onto the top of the counter to use it as a seat.

"Not just mine. It was used by the heavenly hosts. When we would come and stay to watch creation, we stayed here."

"But you guys are all angels... What would you guys need all of this stuff for?"

Michael handed Elaine a handful of violet berries and said, "I may be an angel, but I require food and rest like any other living being. We, too, are part of creation." He took a moment to eat some of the berries and continued, "Granted, I need far less than a human, but without sustenance, I would grow weak just like any living being."

Sure Fire | Michaeli Tom

"Wait, you said that this was the basement. Where is the actual resting place?" Elaine asked, trying hard to remember if she had seen it as they ran.

Michael sighed deeply and replied, "It was destroyed."

"Oh no, that is awful. It must have been beautiful if this was the basement. Was there an accident?"

"No. It was purposefully destroyed. It was done to send a message of... displeasure," Michael said with a tinge of sadness in his masculine voice.

"Who would have done such a thing?"

"There is only one being, one full of vengeance and hate. After the fall, Lucifer tried to get back into heaven, but the Creator had sealed her out. Purgatory was the closest that she could ever get to us. She was so enraged... She began destroying and corrupting everything in her path. Humans say that hell hath no fury like a woman scorned. Once Lucifer has been scorned, she lashes out with such wild viciousness that she destroys all in her path."

Elaine shuddered at the thought of truly being caught by this beast. She still was unable to remember what she had done to attract the attention of the Mistress of Misery, but it had already been done.

"I'm doomed." Elaine breathed out.

"We are not doomed. We have the protection and strength provided by the Creator. He would never abandon us now," Michael said while making Elaine meet his gaze. "When they fell from grace, they were cut off from any and all aide from the Creator. There is no way for them to prevail while we remain in the protection of Yahweh."

"The fall… you have said that before. What does that mean?" Elaine needed to talk of something else before she began hyperventilating.

"The day that Lucifer and her followers fell from grace," Michael solemnly replied.

"That must have been awful for you," Elaine said in her gentlest tone.

"It was. I lost brothers, sisters, and most of all, I lost you." His hoarse voice was filled with a pain that was blatantly evident in his eyes.

"I don't understand. How was I lost from you in the fall? I didn't even exist yet," Elaine said confusedly.

"Yes, you did." Michael took a deep breath and looked at Elaine. He studied her eyes for a moment, searching for any form of recognition or understanding, looking for the words he needed to use to make her remember, but every idea that came to him would never work. They needed time to get to know each other again. Maybe if he did something that she recognized, she would remember.

Chapter 6

glimpses

"Let's take a walk," Michael suggested as he began putting away all of the different containers of food and other supplies.

"When?"

"Now. We could get some fresh air and continue our conversation."

Elaine looked at Michael confused and replied, "It must be pitch black outside by now. Not to mention the devil dogs that are hunting us. How long will the perfume from these flowers mask our scents from them?"

Michael looked at his folded hands as his arms rested on top of the counter. After a moment of thought, he replied, "You are right. We should rest now while we can. In the morning, we will have to fetch water and find more Helleborus blooms."

"So, do we just sleep on the ground?" Elaine was becoming a bit nervous about sleeping in such close proximity to Michael. She had slept near him at the campfire their first night in purgatory and literally slept in his arms as he carried her through the woods. Yet, purposefully going to sleep in the same room felt more intimate. It made her feel uneasy and extremely vulnerable.

"Hey, what's going on? You have turned white as a ghost," Michael said, noticing Elaine's shift into panic mode.

"Nothing." Elaine deflected.

"Listen, there are some pillows and huge duvets that used to be stored in the cabinets along the east wall. I will get you a bunch of pillows and blankets so that you are comfortable. Then I will get myself some and sleep on the other side of the room. How does that sound?"

Elaine looked up into Michael's calm, azure eyes and felt a little comfort. She knew that he would never hurt her, but knowing something and believing it to be true are completely different things. There was still so much Elaine didn't know about Michael, and so much distrust of others formed through her mortal life.

"I can help get everything," Elaine quietly uttered.

"Sounds like a plan, then," Michael said with a sideways grin. "Come on, they should be over here."

What looked like a beautifully decorated wall to Elaine was actually an intricately designed floor-to-ceiling cabinet. Michael pressed on the wall, and two large doors opened up to multiple shelves of brilliantly white pillows, sheets, and duvets.

Elaine smiled widely as she gazed upon all of the squishy, comfortable-looking bedding. She was sure that she could make an insanely cozy pallet to sleep on. Excitedly, she began grabbing pillow after pillow and carrying it to the far side of the island. Once she had completely covered the floor with massive feather pillows, she grabbed two heavy duvets out of the cabinet and placed them both on top of her little pillow bed. She returned to the cabinet for two more pillows to actually use to sleep. One for her head, and the other she would hold tight like a teddy bear for comfort.

After she had finished plumping and rearranging everything to her liking, she stood up to find where Michael had decided to sleep. She saw him with one pillow and a blanket at the foot of the stairs. She looked at the now nearly empty cabinet and wondered why he didn't grab anything else.

"Are you sure you are going to be comfortable with only one pillow?"

Michael looked over to her mountain of bedding and chuckled to himself. "I wasn't sure if you were going to need anything else."

Elaine was now used to him poking fun at her and decided to say, "Hmmmm, nope. I am going to be fine. You are welcome to what is left."

Michael noticed the triumphant smirk on Elaine's face, and it warmed his heart.

"Everyone, watch out. Elaine has got some jokes," he teased her again.

"I do, and I am hilarious. Now, if you are ready for bed, I must bid you goodnight," Elaine said as she situated herself into her little slice of heaven.

"Goodnight, dear," Michael's deep voice sent a shiver down Elaine's spine.

Michael began speaking in his celestial language, and the light from the three crystal vases dimmed to where there was just enough light to see by.

"Hey, Michael?" Elaine said in a small voice.

"Yes?"

"I have been trying to remember my life... I know it wasn't much of a life, but it would still help me if I could remember what happened. I don't even remember how I died."

"Elaine, I don't want to be the one to tell..."

"No, you don't have to tell me anything." Elaine interrupted him. "I just want to tell you the things I remember, and you can tell me if it actually happened or if it's some twisted thought from our angry stalker."

"Must we do this right now?" Michael asked, hoping to change her mind.

"I can't sleep, and it has been plaguing my mind. Please?" Elaine begged.

"Fine."

"I was an orphan. My parents died when I was young, and I didn't have anyone after my grandmother died, did I?"

"No. Your family was gone."

"People hated me. I never had many close friends. I was alone for most of my life." Elaine took a deep breath as the memories assaulted her heart.

"Elaine, they didn't hate you. They didn't understand you." Michael tried to comfort her.

"Ha, I was always an outcast. Left out, uninvited, ridiculed, take your pick of how you see it; it never changed. I never knew what I was doing wrong for everyone to count me out." Elaine's throat was tightening painfully as she tried to speak.

"They didn't understand how someone could go through everything that you went through and yet remain unbroken."

"They obviously didn't look close enough then."

"Elaine…"

"It's all right. I was married, wasn't I?"

"Yes." Michael snarled.

"What is wrong with you?" Elaine asked, very intrigued as to what could have upset Michael.

"Nothing," he curtly replied once again.

"Convincing," Elaine sarcastically said. "Did I have any children?"

"No. Sure Fires are incapable of having children," Michael answered in that same grumpy tone.

"He wasn't good to me, was he? I remember him being such a sweet man when I met him, but something happened. He became dark and cold. I just thought that he figured out whatever it was that the entire world knew already. I wasn't fit to be loved."

"He treated you horribly because that is who he was! It had nothing to do with you!" Michael sat up so that he could look into Elaine's eyes as he said, "You are light and kindness. You were good in an evil world! Of course, they would hate you for that. They couldn't continue in their darkness when you shone so brightly."

"I had wanted to give up so many times." Elaine choked on her words as the emotions that had built up tried to suffocate her.

"I know you did. The fact that you didn't shows your resilience to the ways of darkness," Michael said, trying to look into her eyes so that she would know he was telling the truth, but Elaine kept her eyes focused down at her entwined hands.

Sure Fire | Michaeli Tom

"I don't know what would have happened to me if I hadn't been given my Bible. The relationship that I was able to build with Jesus was the only thing that kept me afloat in the sea of hate that threatened to swallow me whole. Jesus was the only person that never left me. The only one that I knew loved me for who I was. He was the only thing that gave me peace and rest when everyone else said I never deserved anything aside from pain." Elaine finished with a sniffle.

"Well, now you are free from them. Now, we get to join the Creator in heaven. You did everything that you were meant to do."

"Was I a failure?"

"No! Why would you even think that?"

"I just don't understand why any of this is happening. If I did my job, why are we stranded here? Why have I once again been exiled?" Elaine asked with exhaustion in her voice.

"I am not sure, but I know that we have not been exiled. I was sent to retrieve you. I know that we will make it out of this, and I know that the Creator is going to protect us from any harm," Michael said stoically.

"How could you know this?"

"Because I know the Creator, and I know you. Despite everything that is going on, you never give up. Together, we are stronger, and I will never leave you."

Elaine replayed those words in her mind. She was tired and emotionally depleted. She knew in her heart that God would never abandon her, and now she also had a friend. She would live through this and be stronger because of it.

"We really should get some rest now." Michael's deep voice rang out.

Elaine nodded her head and was enveloped by her mounds of bedding. The warm glow the lights gave off was peaceful to Elaine's worried mind. The warm light was easing her mind as the pillows and blankets soothed her body. Finally feeling safe, Elaine closed her eyes and was soon fast asleep.

....

"Good morning, class. How was everyone's Christmas?" Elaine said to a room full of children aged six to seventeen. She was standing in an old white schoolhouse, and all of the children addressed her as Miss White. She was dressed in a simple, brown, long-sleeved dress that flowed to her ankles. A white apron with three small pockets adorned her waist. Pencils, scissors, chalk, and twine were neatly stored in the apron, ready for her to use as she taught her eager students.

The children all began spouting fanciful stories and grand tales about their time away from the schoolhouse. Elaine laughed as she enjoyed every inventive story the children told her. Elaine felt how full her heart was as she spoke to the eleven students in her schoolhouse.

She knew their names, faces, personalities, and families. She could tell what they were going to say before they even said anything. She loved the relationships that she had built with her students and was forever grateful for moving to the rural town in Oklahoma.

"All right, everyone, settle in. Today, we are going to be learning multiplication tables. Get your workbooks out so that we may

begin," she heard herself say as she turned to the large chalkboard that was placed at the front of the small classroom.

Suddenly, everything dropped, and when Elaine reopened her eyes, she was running through rugged tents. Wounded men were being rushed to doctors and nurses to receive care.

"Amenez-le moi! Tu dois etre rapide!" *Elaine shouted to the man carrying a young boy who was bleeding from his chest.*

"Que lui est-il arrive?" *she shouted over the ruckus of the makeshift hospital.*

"C'etatit les allemands!" *the man replied.*

She quickly began cleaning the bleeding gash that had been torn through the boy's right pectoral muscle. She was working as quickly as she possibly could to stop the bleeding and save this young man's life. Blood began soaking into Elaine's apron as she continued to diligently work on her patient. When she turned her head to call for additional supplies, three German planes flew over the makeshift hospital.

This great war was ravishing the countryside and everyone that was stranded on it. She was about to call out to the surgeon when everything spun out of control, and darkness enveloped her once again.

A faint light sprung to life at the end of a long hallway. Elaine began to creep through the darkness to find its source as she neared the small, lit room at the other end. There, she was able to hear a hushed whisper.

"Yes, this is Mrs. Howell," said a gentle elderly voice.

"Yes... that is my daughter and son-in-law... What hap... a car wreck? Are they all right? Which hospital do I need to... Dead?"

Elaine's young mind couldn't understand what was happening, but she was sure she didn't want to hear any more of this conversation. She began to run back to her room with tears falling down her face. Her parents had died when she was just seven years old. This memory she knew intimately, and she wanted to see something else; anything else. Yet, it was as if the wretchedness of this life was being thrust upon her once more.

She was sent to live with her elderly grandmother, who then got sick and passed away when she was thirteen. Having no other relations, she was sent to different homes and families. Trouble after trouble found its way into her life, and then she crossed paths with a young man named Jeremiah.

Time and time again, she would see glimpses of lives she could feel but not fully remember. She tried to cling to each as it passed before her eyes, yet each fled as quickly as it came. Over and over again, she saw places and faces that gnawed at her mind. Trying in vain to unlock everything that had been kept from her waking mind.

When Elaine woke with a start, she felt as if she had spent the night studying for an exam that she would inevitably fail. Her heart felt as if it were going to pound out of her chest, and her mind felt overworked and completely depleted. She lay in the comfort of her warm blankets for a while, just staring at the dimly lit ceiling, trying in vain to calm her racing heart.

She continued to try and remember anything that would help her relate to the visions that plagued her mind. She knew the faces, sights, smells, and voices that continued to ring in her ears. Voices that were calling out to her as if they were trying to pull her from the darkness and reveal themselves to her.

The harder she tried to focus, the more she failed and the more she wanted to give up. She was becoming so frustrated with herself. Why was she seeing all of these people? Why did she wholeheartedly believe that these visions were real? Why was she trying to remember something that may turn out to just be a dream?

So many questions with no answers. It seemed to Elaine that all she would receive in this place would be more questions. The only constant she had to rely on was her confusion.

She sat up and looked to where her companion peacefully slept. He looked as if nothing in the world could bother him in his slumber. Elaine tried to be annoyed that he was sleeping so soundly, but as she studied his calm form, she saw how undeniably handsome he was.

She didn't want to disturb him, but it was time for answers. All of her questions were about to be answered. No more will she allow the answers to be withheld from her. She would learn why she was here and not in heaven. She would understand who she truly was to Michael. Most importantly, she would finally get to the bottom of why Lucifer was planning to carry out her utter annihilation.

Time to wake the crazy angel, Elaine thought to herself.

She pulled back the top duvet and set her bare feet on the cold hardwood floor. For a second, she considered covering herself back up and waiting until Michael woke up. No, she wanted answers, and she was going to get them.

She stood up and looked at the three jars still sitting in the middle of the island. "I don't know how to speak to you, but I remember that your name is Seraphina. Could you please shine bright enough to light the room for me?"

Seraphina glowed brightly for Elaine. The room was lit, and Elaine felt sure of herself. She crossed the room to stand next to her only hope for understanding her situation. She wasn't sure how to go about waking him.

"Psst… Michael," she called in a whisper.

Michael stirred slightly and rubbed his nose. He rolled onto his left side so that his broad back was turned to Elaine.

"Ugh, Michael," Elaine said a bit louder.

Not even a single twitch. No movements at all. Elaine was beginning to get upset and decided to nudge his shoulder this time.

"Michael," she loudly said while grabbing his right shoulder.

"What is it? What's wrong? Who's here?" Michael shouted as he sprung to his feet. He faced the stairs and pushed Elaine behind his large form.

Everything happened so quickly that Elaine froze. The amount of power that radiated from Michael as he prepared to defend Elaine from the non-existent threat terrified her. Elaine began to pull away from him. She was scared of what would happen if she made him lose his temper.

She learned what some men were capable of in her life on earth. Michael was far stronger, faster, and just all around more than any mortal man. Elaine tried to shrink into herself. Her heart was pounding painfully in her chest as she backed away from Michael.

"I'm sorry... I... I... I sh... shouldn't have touched you. I'm sorry." Elaine stuttered as she stared at her feet. Tears threatened to spill down her frightened face.

She could see Michael turn and face her. He took a deep breath and stepped closer to her. Elaine flinched and steadied herself for whatever would happen next.

She was shocked when she felt his strong arms wrap around her in a wonderfully soothing hug. His left arm pulled her close to his warm embrace while his right hand gently caressed her hair. They stayed in that position until Elaine relaxed into the embrace. Michael took his right hand and raised Elaine's small face to look into her eyes.

"You never need to fear me. I was worried that we had been found. I was simply trying to protect you." Michael's deep voice was incredibly sincere and reassuring. "I am so sorry that I frightened you. I never want you to be scared of me. I am truly sorry, my love."

Elaine's throat closed painfully whenever she tried to respond to him. She could see that Michael was different, but the scars that she carried were deep. She nodded her head to communicate that she believed him and that she accepted his apology.

Michael took a step back and cleared his throat. "Would you like to go on that walk now?"

Chapter 7

getting closer

Elaine watched as Michael walked to the island at the far end of the room. He spoke gently to the other two lights, and light softly filled the entire space. Michael grabbed a large bag and began placing different pouches and containers inside. After a few minutes, he closed up the bag and stood to face Elaine.

"Are you ready to head out?"

Elaine nodded her head. She looked up into Michael's calm, expressive eyes and saw nothing but warmth towards her. She forced a small smile to settle on her lips as she waited for Michael to take the lead.

They walked up the stairs in a comfortable silence. Each not knowing how to approach the other. Each desperately wanting the other to be the one to break through the distance that this silence had created.

They reached the top of the staircase, and Michael spoke to the walls, willing them to open. The bright rays of the morning sun were a vast contrast to the small lights of the safe place.

The trees surrounding them had a dense layer of fog that had settled in between them. It was as if the surroundings thought it was suitable to mirror exactly what Elaine was feeling inside.

"First, we should make our way down to the river. Helleborus flowers can normally be found along the banks of the river. While we are there, we can wash off and fill up a few canteens as we prepare for the last leg of our journey."

Elaine simply nodded at Michael's suggested plan. Not knowing what to add to the conversation, she chose to fall in line until her heart had enough time to get settled down.

Michael started leading them down a large, smooth path through the woods. The path was straight for the most part. A few slight turns here and there, and all the while, it led downward toward a valley.

When they neared the bottom of the valley, Elaine could faintly hear the rush of water. She knew just by the sound of the river that it was going to be large. Out of the corner of her eye, she spotted a small cluster of black flowers. She stopped and went to pick as many as she could find.

"That is a good find. I walked straight past them." Michael praised her.

Elaine smiled a small, hollow smile and said, "Well, I know we need them. I thought I may as well grab them while they are next to me."

"I'm glad you did. We will need as many as we can get to last us the next two days. Here, put them into this bag."

Michael handed Elaine a dark purple bag that had golden embroidered vines on it. The fabric felt like the softest velvet

Elaine had ever felt, and it closed with golden drawstrings. Together, they were able to gather enough flowers to fill the bag halfway.

"We will need a couple more to make sure we have enough, but this is a great start. If you see any more, let me know," Michael said as they continued down the path to the river.

Elaine was lost in admiring the beauty of the large hills and foliage around her. She was especially mesmerized by the large waterfall that was pouring over the path they were walking down. She walked under the flowing waters and kept watching them flow as she continued walking. Not paying attention to her steps, she almost walked off the path. Michael grabbed her tightly before she could fall into the rushing river below and held her closely until his heart calmed.

"Please be careful. I couldn't bear to lose you."

"I am all right," Elaine said, a little shaken. She took a step back and held her arms out for him to see that she was, in fact, in one piece. "See, you don't have to worry."

Michael looked her over and then turned to continue his walk. He walked along the path as it curved to the left around a large willow. The only sounds that could be heard were those of the rushing water and their footsteps as they crushed dry leaves.

Now that Elaine had spoken out loud, the silence between them was almost enough to drive her crazy. Clawing at the back of her mind like the shriek of chalk on a chalkboard. She wanted to ask him every question she had building inside of her since their time together had started. Just as she was about to speak, Michael jumped off the ledge of the path that they had been walking on.

He landed a few feet down next to this bunch of Helleborus blooms. He turned to face Elaine and held his arms out for her to jump to him.

"You can't seriously think I am going to jump to you. We would both get injured," Elaine said defiantly.

"I am more than capable of catching a tiny thing like you. Come on. Jump!"

"There is no way!"

"Don't be a turkey!"

"A what?" Elaine said with a loud bark of laughter.

"Isn't that what the humans call each other when you are being cowardly?" Michael said with a slight look of confusion on his face.

"I am not being cowardly! Wait, are you trying to call me a chicken? What are you three years old?" Elaine said as she continued to laugh.

"Yes, you are a chicken. You are failing to do even a little jump while I am here to help you. That is being a chicken."

"Little jump." Elaine scoffed. "This has to be at least an eight-foot drop. You have to be... What? 6'3" or 6'4". Your arms are stretched out above your head, and it still isn't enough to reach my feet."

"I will catch you. Trust me."

There was a little bit of a challenge in the tone that Michael used. He was trying to goad her into jumping, but Elaine felt as if it were about much more than this moment.

"Fine," Elaine said, choosing to put her trust in Michael. "But if you drop me, so help me, I will smother you in your sleep tonight."

Michael laughed loudly. It was deep and rumbled through his chest like thunder. It was the first time Elaine had ever heard him heartily laugh like this. There was no hint of worry in his eyes or tenseness in his muscles. Simply happy.

Elaine sat at the edge of the path and allowed her feet to dangle off the side. Michael was able to grab her left foot and tugged playfully on it.

"Hey, you have to wait until I am ready!" Elaine chastised him.

He held up his large hands in a show of surrender, "All right, all right. Whenever you are ready."

"Yep… Okay… On the count of three. One, two…" Elaine closed her eyes and shouted, "Three!"

She pushed off the wall and began plunging through the air. The pit of her stomach filled with the feeling of flittering butterfly wings. She squealed out a shout of delight, and within mere moments, she was safely wrapped in Michael's arms. Her feet were still a few inches off of the ground, completely unharmed.

"You were very brave," Michael said with a chuckle.

"I know I was. Now put me down so we can pick these flowers."

Reluctantly, Michael did as she asked, and they began to once again fill up their bag with the flowers they picked. After a few minutes, the entire bag was stuffed full of the sweet blossoms. Task one had been completed, and now they needed to find the river to bathe and get fresh water.

"Follow me. The river should be just around the corner here," Michael said as he began navigating their unmarked path.

When they reached an opening, Elaine saw that this part of the river was wide and calm. A few large boulders sat a small distance away from the slow-moving water's edge. Sheer rock cliffs lined the river on the far side, yet Elaine stood on the small pebbled beach of this massive inlet.

The water was beautifully crystal clear once again, and Elaine was desperate to wash away the sweat and grime from the day before. She took off her shoes and rolled her sleeves and pant legs. When she glanced up, she saw Michael setting his shirt on top of one of the boulders.

The muscles were even more defined than she had initially thought. A large mark was placed between his shoulder blades and spread out across his back and neck. The base of the mark was centered on his spine and looked like a swirling heart with a blocky cross in its center. On top of that rested a five-pointed crown with what looked like an *A* inside of another *A*. Feathered wings spread out from the design and covered his shoulders and flowed down to wrap around his ribs.

She quickly looked away so as not to be caught drooling over this man. She couldn't live with that type of embarrassment. "I didn't know angels could get tattoos." She attempted to distract herself with conversation.

"I don't have a tattoo."

"What do you call that huge design on your back then?"

88   *Sure Fire* | Michaeli Tom

"It is the mark of what I am."

Michael dove into the shallow waters, and when he surfaced, he was facing Elaine, who was still standing on the pebbled shore. He stood up so that the water came up to his stomach. Elaine was fighting herself to stay looking at Michael's face and not his broad chest.

Upon a brief glance at his muscular chest, Elaine noticed a deep red scar that ran from his right collarbone down through his right pec. The scar was thick and splintered as if he were cut in multiple directions.

"I thought you were an angel? Do all angels have this mark? Also, how does an angel end up with a scar?" Elaine asked. She had to busy her mind with conversation in order to save herself from a disaster.

"I am an angel. And no, not all angels have this mark; it displays the type of angel that I am. To get this scar, you must go toe to toe with Lucifer," Michael said with a bit of humor in his voice.

"You tried to take on the devil… by yourself?"

"Yes. I was sent to retrieve Moses' body and…"

"Wait… There is no way that you are *that* Michael. You're trying to tell me that you are the Archangel Michael? There is no way," Elaine said with pure disbelief in her voice.

"Do you know of another angel named Michael?" he asked with a hint of confusion in his voice.

"I don't know… I met tons of people named Michael in my life."

Sure Fire | Michaeli Tom

"That isn't how names work among angels. There is one name for one angel, each given to us by the Creator. My name is Michael."

"That is insane! So, you were sent to retrieve Moses' body… that sounds so weird… and ended up fighting and getting hurt by Lucifer in the process?" Elaine's eyes were as large as saucers as she waited for Michael to tell her the story as it actually happened.

Michael walked to the shore and sat at the water's edge, leaving his feet in the warm water.

"Are you sure you can handle this? You look as if you are about to pass out already," Michael said as he gestured to her painfully excited face.

An instant frown appeared in place of her large smile, and her eyebrows drew together in a scowl. "I was excited to hear it, but now you're being rude."

"I was just making sure you wanted the whole story. Moses was the only person in the history of mankind to ever stand in the actual physical presence of the Creator multiple times. He was the only person to be not only spiritually close but physically close to the Creator. When they were on the mount, and Yahweh showed Moses his back, it changed Moses. It imprinted a part of His glory in Moses' body."

"What about Adam? He walked with the Creator while he lived in the garden. Surely, that was more contact than Moses." Elaine asked enthusiastically.

"Yes, they walked together. Then, when the creation decided to follow the serpent and disobey the rule of the Creator, they fell. Cut off from the glory of Yahweh, just as the fallen had been cut off from His presence."

"Jesus is God and spent years among people. Why would none of them work?"

"Jesus is God made flesh. He was meant to encounter people and have them encounter Him. He had relinquished parts of Himself so that he could live a human life. When Moses sat in the presence of the Father, His glory washed over him, making him glow as we do."

"And Lucifer wanted the body because it was glowing?" Elaine asked, extremely invested in the story.

"She was after the sliver of God's glory that had been trapped inside of it. She thought that she could somehow use it to gain some of the power or abilities that only Yahweh possesses. As Moses was a faithful servant of the Creator, I was sent to retrieve him to ensure Lucifer could not experiment on his form nor twist his likeness to deceive those who trusted him. I was sent on the Creator's authority, but I am still not able to overpower Lucifer on my own."

"Why not? I thought she was cut off from the Creator's power."

"She was. That doesn't change what she is on her own. We were locked in a standoff, waiting for the other to back down or make a mistake. She began taunting me, accusing me of betraying her by leading the heavenly army that cast them all out. She tried to make me feel remorseful for 'being the reason that she and so many of my brothers and sisters are barred from their rightful homes.' She said, 'They all were looking for you to help lead them. They were depending on you to help them, but you betrayed us all. I bet you rejoiced with Him as we fell from our rightful place.' On and on she went until I stepped forward in anger and on my own authority, and that is when she stabbed a large knife into my chest. She missed my heart, but she twisted and turned the knife in my shoulder to make sure I would be too wounded to fight. I fell to the ground while she threw back her head in spiteful laughter. In her moment of pride, I crawled to Moses' body and prayed for help. God removed us both from the earth and out of her reach. The scar was left as a reminder not to act out of anger."

"That is so cool! Not that you got hurt or anything, but I have grown up hearing that story... That was you! That is absolutely mind-blowing."

Michael sat quietly with an amused look on his face as Elaine expressed how amazing that story was to her. Suddenly, Elaine's face changed into one of confusion or contemplation.

"Wait, why would she think that any of this was your fault?" Elaine asked, barely above a whisper.

"She and I were extremely close before the fall. Sometimes, a few of the other heavenly hosts went as far as to call us twins due to our close friendship. She was my best friend, and I would have done almost anything for her. Near the end, she would always ask me if I loved her, if I still loved her, if we were loyal to one another. I always responded the same, that, of course, I loved her and that I would always love her. When she rose up her army, I was so lost. How could she do this? Why would she do this? I was standing before the Creator when she came looking for a fight. She looked for me to join beside her, but I could not. I loved her, but I would never betray my God for anyone. When I called for the hosts to come to my aide in opposing them, the look of betrayal on her face was all too evident. She forced me to choose. She didn't have to do any of this, yet she did. Yahweh cast them all out of the heavens and took their ability to gain any footholds here. My brothers and sisters that fell were looking for me to join them, but they should have known that I would never betray my Creator."

When Michael finished speaking, there was a silence that settled uncomfortably between the two. Silence weighed heavily upon Elaine's shoulders as she tried to understand that type of jealousy and hate.

"She tried to use your love for her to blind you from what was right. You never lost sight of what was good, and you should be proud of what you did. Choosing to do the right thing, even if it costs you someone that you love, will never be wrong. I am proud of you, Michael. It must have been incredibly hard for you to do, and I am so proud of your choice," Elaine said in complete earnestness.

Michael looked into her emerald eyes and found nothing but pure compassion and care for him there. Elaine was comforting him in his time of need. She was proud of him, and nothing could have made him feel more reassured of his actions than that.

He rumbled a very sincere thank-you. Emotions were filling his heart to the point that it felt as if it would burst open. He remained trapped looking into her eyes because there he found concern for his well-being and his emotions. There still was no recognition of him from their past, but he was sure that Elaine was finally beginning to genuinely care for him again.

Sure Fire | Michaeli Tom

After a few more moments, the intensity had grown too much for Elaine, and she turned her head to face the water and cleared her throat. She needed a few minutes to process everything she had heard and how seeing Michael look defeated stirred up something deep in her heart. She couldn't bear to see him look so overwhelmed. She decided that she needed a few moments alone.

"Well, seeing as how you are the only one who has gotten to bathe, it looks like it is my turn. I'm going to need you to go somewhere and fill up the canteens so that I can get an actual bath."

A look of amusement crossed Michael's face before he nodded and replied, "As you wish."

"I used to love a movie that said that. I don't remember much, but I remember that," Elaine said with a fond smile.

"I know. That's why I said it," Michael said as he slipped on a clean black shirt and picked up the bag of supplies. He reached into a side pocket, where he grabbed a glass bottle that he then handed to Elaine. "It is a Helleborus soap; use it to wash your hair and body. It will cover your scent far longer this way."

"As you wish," Elaine said with a slight smirk.

Michael smiled brightly at Elaine before he nodded at her and turned to walk a bit upstream.

Elaine could hardly believe she said that to him. Especially since he knew what she was talking about. The farm boy in the movie would always say "As you wish" in place of "I love you." She knew that she had indirectly told Michael that she loved him, and she was scared because she truly felt as if she were starting to.

As she waded out into the water to cleanse her body, her mind was running in circles. On one hand, Michael was this incredibly intimidating figure who could snap her like a twig. On the other hand, he had been nothing but helpful, kind, and reassuring through everything that they had been through. He had started to answer all of her questions and had been completely honest with all of his answers. He had done nothing but save her from harm and her own lack of expertise in the wilderness. He also continues to find ways to keep her from being found by those who would love nothing more than to kill her.

The feeling of safety and comfort that she received from Michael's presence surpassed anything that she had ever known. Her life on earth had been anything but easy. Relationships were always hard, and she had to learn how to shield her heart from everyone. Now, she found herself wanting to let this person in, but the boundaries that she was forced to create still remained.

"Elaine," she heard Michael shout from a short distance.

"Yes?"

"Are you ready to head back?"

"No, sorry. I guess I have been a little lost in thought. Give me a second to rinse and dress," Elaine said as she began to rush to get everything done.

"I caught some fish and was wondering if you would like to have dinner tonight. We could eat and talk, and I was thinking we could watch the stars for a little while." Michael continued to shout so that they could have a conversation despite the distance between them.

"Are you asking me out on a date?" Elaine teased.

"Dates are a mortal thing. I am asking you to spend the evening with me."

"That would be a date." Elaine couldn't help herself as she teased him once more.

"Fine. Will you allow me to prepare a date for you this evening?" Michael conceded.

"I guess I will allow it this once," Elaine said stoically. She was attempting to hide her nervousness with humor. In reality, she was equal parts excited and terrified for what the evening held for her. "Wait, are you sure that it would be safe? We may need to have a rain check," she said in hopes of giving herself a little more time.

"I will take care of everything. I promise; everything will be perfectly safe," Michael shouted back in response.

Elaine finished washing her hair in the river and began to dress quickly in the clothes that had been set out for her. She never even saw Michael put these out for her, but she was grateful to be in clean clothes. She had a fresh, heather grey long-sleeved shirt, black jeans, and the coziest socks she had felt in a while.

Chapter 8

first date

The rest of the day seemed to fly by in a blur for Elaine. Michael was running up and down the stairs, checking cabinets for different things, and carrying the things he found up the stairs and out of their temporary home.

Every time Elaine asked if she could help with one thing or another, Michael would tell her that he wanted to do it himself and that she should relax. The more she was told to relax, the more she found herself incapable of relaxing. She needed to do something, or she was sure she would end up losing her mind in this enclosed space.

Elaine began to open up all of the cabinets that she could find and look for anything that could be useful in their journey that would start in two days' time. She found rope, bandages, a couple of jars of the healing tonic that she had taken before, three large silver knives, and a small sky-blue bag that reminded her of an early-age book bag.

She set about organizing all of her findings into the large part of the bag. She put the jars of tonic in the bottom of the bag after she had wrapped them in a thick sheet to prevent them from breaking. Next, she placed the bandages and rope on top, as they were relatively light and provided extra cushioning for the glass jars. The knives, she placed in the side pocket of her bag so that they were easier to find.

Once everything was placed into her bag, she noticed that she had quite a bit of extra room. She returned to the island and looked for a couple of tins of the mixed nuts and berries. She also grabbed a block of cheese that had been wrapped in a purple cheesecloth.

Satisfied with her finds and the organization of her pack, Elaine began walking around the room, picking up everything that she had moved or discarded earlier. She folded up the blankets that she and Michael had used the night before and stacked the pillows neatly along the far wall of the space. She was just about to finish cleaning off the island when Michael walked down the steps.

"I hope you're hungry," he said with a small crooked grin on his face.

"I am starving! I bet I could eat an entire horse by myself."

Michael's face quirked in a confused look, and then he chuckled before he replied, "Well, I hope that you approve of the non-horse meal I have prepared for you."

"Time will tell." Elaine joked. "Where are we eating? I didn't see you bring anything down."

"I have set everything up for us to eat outside. I thought that you would want to get out of here and stretch your legs for a while."

"Do you think that we will be safe out in the open?" Elaine couldn't keep the worry from seeping into her voice.

"I have taken care of everything. I need you to trust me."

Elaine nodded her head after a moment of consideration. Michael had taken care of her up to this point. If he told her that she would be safe tonight, then she chose to believe him.

"Thank you. Now, I know it isn't much, but for a last-minute date in exile, I think it will do the trick," Michael said in a cocky tone.

"I'm sure it will be lovely," Elaine said as she followed Michael out of the safety of their shelter and into the open night air.

The cool night air washed over Elaine and calmed her worries. The gentle breeze floated through the trees and caressed Elaine's face as it brought the sweet floral scent of wildflowers and pine to her nose. She closed her eyes to take in a deep breath of the enchantingly fresh scent.

The coolness of the breeze brushing the exposed portion of her neck reminded Elaine of her home in Colorado. Standing on the porch with a steaming cup of coffee in the morning, just waiting for the sun to peak up over the mountains. The comforting shiver that the cold brought often made her feel like an ice princess. Her mother always called her a polar bear when she was young due to her love of the winter air.

After all the memories had passed, Elaine opened her eyes and looked up at the rainbow of colors peeping through the canopy of leaves. She was trying so hard to get a good look at the stars, but the branches and leaves were in her way.

"If you're ready to go, I think you will like where our dinner is set out for us," Michael said in an unsure tone. It seemed to

Sure Fire | Michaeli Tom

Elaine as if Michael were nervous. If Elaine didn't notice the unsettled look in his eyes earlier, she did now.

"Lead the way," Elaine said with a small smile.

Michael paused to push a lock of hair behind Elaine's ear. The simple but overly affectionate motion melted Elaine's heart. She flashed a brilliant smile up at the man before her.

"You never cease to amaze me… " Michael said in a deep, rumbling tone. He took a deep breath as if he wanted to say more but couldn't. "Now, why don't we go and eat?"

"That sounds nice," Elaine agreed in a small voice, due to her fear of any emotion flowing out too strongly if she spoke clearly.

Michael took Elaine by the hand and began leading her down a different path than the one that they took this morning to the river. This path was winding and had many stones and roots to trip over. If it weren't for Michael guiding her through the different steps, Elaine was sure she would have fallen many times over.

They followed the path around a bend to the left, up and over a tree that served as a bridge to a flowing creek, down a small slope, and finally over a small grass-covered hill. As they came to the top of the hill, Elaine saw the beautiful clearing that was before her. Flowers and grasses grew wild and free. A large sheet was laid out in the middle of the field with plates and containers of goodies spread neatly across the middle with Helleborus blooms scattered throughout. Small lights had been placed around the sheet so that they would be able to see all the delicious foods that were set out for their dinner.

When Elaine looked up, she was dazzled by the kaleido-scopic stars. Rainbows of color were flowing out of each star and illuminating the sky in a way that Elaine could never have imagined. Accompanying the alluring stars were three small moons floating in harmony with one another. They seemed to be forming a perfect triangle in the sky. Maybe an arrow pointing the way home for the wayward travelers that used to traverse these woods.

"I have never seen anything as incredibly beautiful as this! This is amazing! I am just at a loss for words. Is this not breath-taking?" Wonder filled the tones of Elaine's soft voice.

"It certainly is." Michael agreed but never removed his eyes from her shining face.

A blush tinged Elaine's cheek as she reeled from his heart-felt compliment.

"Come, let's eat before the food gets cold," Michael said as he turned to walk toward the impromptu picnic.

As the two picked their places to sit, Elaine's eyes were as huge as her stomach, which growled loudly at the sight of so many different options.

"How did you do all of this?" Elaine asked in amazement.

"I had caught the fish in the river and cooked them over a fire as I gathered the rest of what you see here. Most of it was in the basement, but the rest is easy to find if you know where to look," he said with a triumphant look on his face.

"Dear God, thank You for this food. May it nourish our bodies so that we are capable of carrying out Your commands. In Jesus' name, Amen," Elaine said quietly before she grabbed a piece of fish and began eating.

Michael sat in wonder as he watched Elaine simply be. It had been such a long time since he had seen her be so carefree. This is how it was supposed to be from now on, and he would not let anything happen to change this.

Elaine groaned in delight as she ate the fish that Michael had cooked. "I don't know if this is delicious or if I was just so hungry that I would eat anything!" she giggled when she saw the look Michael shot her over that comment.

"I'll have you know; I know exactly how you like your fish, and I am an incredible chef," Michael said proudly.

"Tell me how you know how I like my fish." Elaine challenged.

"I have told you," Michael replied with a certain sadness in his voice.

"You have not. You said that you would explain, but that still hasn't fully happened." Elaine countered as she reached for more of the delicious fire-roasted fish.

"Where do you want me to begin?" Michael asked.

"At the very beginning. I want to know everything. Please." Elaine softened her tone as she looked up into Michael's blue eyes.

"Fine, but you will have to allow me to finish the story before you break in with any questions. Deal?"

"How do you know that I would..."

Michael shot her an incredulous look through his eyelashes, his right eyebrow raised in accusation.

Elaine stopped mid-sentence and huffed out, "Fine!"

Pleased with her somewhat agreement, he took a deep breath and started speaking.

"When Yahweh began creation, the heavenly hosts were breathed into existence on the second day. We were there with Him as He began creating the most incredible things out of nothing at all. The new colors, sounds, landscapes, plants, birds, fish, animals, and the way everything was working in harmony with one another amazed us all. Everything was spoken into existence as we were. Everything rejoicing and praising the Creator for the works that He had completed. Then, on the sixth day, He said aloud, 'As it was recorded in Genesis 1:26, "Let us make man in our image, after our likeness."' This statement turned every head in the heavens. He then proceeded to take the dirt and form man, sculpting and reforming until He was pleased. He took the time to mold this new creation into what He wanted it to be. Piece by piece, He worked until He breathed life into the new creation. It was made in His image, as He had stated, but was lacking in all areas. This new creation was not as perfect as He is. It was less powerful and yet full of the same creative wonder that sets Him apart from us."

"Wow! So, man was the only thing that He actually was involved in forming? He didn't form the angels?" Elaine asked, unable to help herself.

"No, he didn't form us. He spoke us, and we were. He made man with free will as all angels had been and set them as a demonstration of sorts for all of the heavenly hosts. Some never cared for the humans, others were losing interest, and others despised you for the attention the Creator was giving to your kind. God knew that if we were to stay engaged with what was happening on earth, a part of ourselves would have to be invested."

Sure Fire | Michaeli Tom

"Ummm, is there anything to drink? I am so sorry; I am not trying to interrupt, but I am trying really hard not to choke." Elaine rushed out.

Michael burst out laughing, which startled Elaine. "You have always done as you pleased, haven't you?" Michael said as he continued to chuckle.

Elaine was completely shocked by his reaction and felt as if she should apologize. "I'm sorry... I am really enjoying your story, but my throat is getting really dry, and I thought you might have something." Her cheeks were flaming red, showing her embarrassment.

"I do. Here, drink this," Michael said as he pulled out a large cut glass decanter and handed it to Elaine.

"This isn't going to knock me unconscious again, is it?" Elaine narrowed her eyes playfully at him as he raised one eyebrow in a challenging way.

"Are you still upset about that? No, it isn't going to do anything other than hydrate you. It is just some of the water we got from the river. I also brought some wine that I found in the shelter and thought you may like some."

She took a large drink of the water and said, "You would be right."

Elaine poured herself a small glass of the wine and drank a sip. It was the most delicious wine she had ever tasted. The incredibly dark liquid was rich and perfectly smooth. After a few more sips, she cleared her throat and asked, "Are you going to finish your story?"

He was still grinning at her, and it was beginning to make her feel utterly ridiculous.

"Thank you," she shyly stated.

"You're very welcome," he said with the same quirky grin. "Now, should I continue, or do you require anything else, princess?"

"I am sure I will be fine. You should be set to continue," she said, showing a bit of her sassy side.

He gave a little bow of his head and picked up where he had been. "The Creator knew that if we were going to stay invested in the lives of humans, there would need to be a piece of us in the new creation. So... He took half of our soul and placed it into our mortal counterpart."

"What? How would that keep you interested and not resentful? Half of your soul was taken from you and given to something else. How were you okay with that?"

"Because mine was given to you."

"I don't understand."

"No, I don't suppose you do," Michael said with a small sigh. After a moment of searching Elaine's eyes for an answer that she would understand, Michael said, "I, like most angels, instantly fell in love with my soulmate. When I was charged with protecting you, I couldn't have been happier. I would be there to watch you learn, grow, change, and decide how to live your life. I would be there to help guide you through your tough decisions. Most of us were extremely happy to take on this new assignment because it gave us purpose. We were created as warriors but had nothing to fight, nothing to fight for. Your creation gave me my purpose."

"Surely not everyone felt the same way."

"Most of us did, but there were a few that did not. They felt as you have imagined. They viewed it as part of them being taken away from them instead of the gift it was. We finally had a true match for ourselves and for our purpose. When they heard Yahweh tell them that they now had to protect the creation that had 'stolen their soul,' they rose up against Him, and they were cast out."

"They must have been furious."

"They were, but none as furious as Lucifer. She truly believed that she was the one true match for the Creator Himself. When He made a counterpart for her as well, then told her to care for that which had taken half of her soul... she felt as if He had betrayed her. To her, He had forsaken her and matched her with a lesser being as a punishment. She truly believed that she deserved to be paired with the Creator. She wanted to be seen as something that was equal to Him, but there is no such thing on earth nor in all of the heavens."

"So, He made her the ruler of Sheol after she rebelled against him?" Elaine asked, confused.

"She is no more the ruler of Sheol than any of the other poor tormented souls that have been sent there."

"What do you mean? I thought that was her... I don't know... domain, I guess," Elaine said as she grabbed another piece of bread and fish.

"No. Sheol is a place where the Creator has completely removed His presence. There is no light, no love, no kindness, goodness, gentleness, comfort, joy, peace, patience, healing, nor anything that the presence of God contains. Everyone there chose to live a life apart from Him, and that is what He has given them in full. An eternity without a hint of His presence."

"Why did you say they chose to be there? Who would ever choose to go to a place like that?" Elaine felt a shiver run down her spine just thinking about being trapped in such a place. "How could anyone ever choose to go there?" she asked in a small, unsure voice.

"He is a merciful God. He never wanted anyone there. It was created specifically for the deceiver and the fallen angels who chose to raise up and challenge His authority. The humans who will find themselves lost within its devastating confines also have chosen to live apart from Him as a way of rebellion. Most don't even realize that they have made the choice to stay out of heaven until it is too late."

"Okay, I can see why someone would want to get out of going to hell, but why would anyone not take the first opportunity they received to go to heaven?" Elaine asked, dumbfounded that this was even an option.

Michael looked at her with a cautious expression on his handsome face. She could sense a deep sadness in his stormy blue eyes.

"Humans have every day of their life to accept the gift that Christ gave them. If they don't, they choose to remain outside of the paradise that was intended for them. The ones like you chose to go back to earth for the same reason that you did… every single time you were asked. You felt that you could do more for the kingdom of heaven there on earth than you could do by sitting apart from it all. You couldn't sit back and leave people hanging in the balance when you could do something to help them find Christ," Michael said in a very somber yet proud tone.

"How many times have I gone back?" She hated asking, but deep down, she knew she needed to have this question answered.

"One hundred and forty-two times," Michael said without any hesitation.

A little gasp escaped from Elaine's lips as she repeated the number to herself.

"Humans only live their one life and are done. The few that are like you get sent on missions to help the lost souls who are struggling to turn their lives around. Some of your lives were only a few years, some a few days, and others, you lived long, fulfilling lives. No matter what you were born into, your soul shone so brightly that each time, you brought at least one other person to the Creator before you passed. People like you are known as Sure Fires."

Chapter 9

Truth hurts

"Sure Fire." She had heard him talk about them before. Michael had told her that she was a Sure Fire that day in the woods after she had eaten Jerusalem cherries. He said that they had been given a home here because she was a Sure Fire and needed a rest between assignments. He never got back around to explaining what that was supposed to mean.

Elaine was now determined to understand exactly what that meant. "How did I become a Sure Fire?"

"You can't become a Sure Fire. It is what you were created to be. There were only ever a few of you. You would be sent to the place where your spirit was needed most, and you never failed a single mission," he said with a proud smile on his lips.

"So, we were just normal people, and what? What makes us different?"

"None of you are normal people. You were created with a fire inside you that humans don't have. Your connection to the Creator and His Son was far deeper than any human connection. The Spirit could flow freely through you so that it could reach far more people than humanly possible."

"Why do I only remember being human?" Elaine said with disbelief covering her face.

"You never have been human. The strongest angels were gifted with Sure Fire soul-bonds due to the task that was appointed to you. Did you truly believe that you were human?"

"Yes! I grew up on earth. I lived a normal human life. What possible reason would I have for believing that I was anything other than a human?" Elaine felt out of breath and at a loss for words.

"You were a gift to those around you, and you are a gift to me. God only made a few of your kind, and even counting those of them who lost their soul-bound guardian," Michael said with a heaviness added to his deep voice. "In the beginning, Yahweh created the world and everything in it. When He was forming man, He also made the Sure Fires to be a light in the world. You all had been created to show the masses the love of the Creator. You were supposed to be paired with your guardian so that both of you would make a greater impact on the people around you. During the fall, so many were lost. Even those that were supposed to be Sure Fires, a direct line to the glory of God, fell and became Dark Fires. They had become direct lines to everything cruel and evil in the world."

"There were others like me? Did I know any other Sure Fires in my life?" Elaine asked. The excitement in her eyes betrayed her calm tone.

"Your best friend is a Sure Fire. I believe in this past life, you knew her as Destiny. The two of you were always better together," Michael said with a small smile.

Elaine thought about her dearest friend. She was the most beautiful woman Elaine had met in her life. Her outer beauty was amplified by her kind and gentle spirit. She was always encouraging and supportive. She showed up in Elaine's life when she needed her the most.

"I remember her! She was the person who gave me my first Bible. We had met in one of the foster homes and became fast friends. She was being adopted by the foster family, and I was being moved somewhere else. It was her parting gift to me. I cherished that Bible, but I never saw her again." Elaine reflected fondly. A smile situated on her lips and a distant look in her eyes. It was as if she were watching herself relive those memories.

Elaine had just finished packing her few belongings into a small blue duffel bag when she decided to sit on her small bed in the corner of her shared bedroom. Since she became an orphan all those years ago, she had never truly had anything worth keeping. As she sat there looking at the blank, soft pink walls of her room for the last time, she heard a knock at the door.

"I hate that we are losing one another," a small, soft voice said from the doorway.

Elaine turned to see her best friend. She was a petite girl just a few years younger than Elaine. Her dark brown hair flowed over

Sure Fire | Michaeli Tom

her shoulders in soft curls as her soft brown eyes stared at Elaine with a sadness that made Elaine's heart shudder.

"Hey, hey! It's going to be all right. We have been through worse, yeah? I am not sure how we can stay in touch, but I will always be thinking of you. Okay?" Elaine said through a strained voice. She couldn't let Destiny know how badly this separation was going to tear her apart.

"I have something that I want you to have," Destiny said as she walked to her side of the room. She pulled open the bottom drawer of her pine wood cabinet and grabbed a book. "This was my mother's. She used to read it to me before I would go to sleep. She made notes and some small drawings on the pages, but I think they can help you figure out what each story means. It means a lot to me, but so do you. Now, if I know that you both are together… I don't know. It just makes me feel better to know that you will have this."

"Des, I couldn't possibly take your mother's book."

"It isn't just a book; it is her Bible. It can be something that you will remember me by."

"I don't need anything to remember you by, sweet girl. You should keep this. I don't even believe in this stuff. I don't think I would ever read it anyway," Elaine said, trying her best not to offend her sweet friend.

"You may not believe in it now, but this could help you when you truly need it," Destiny said with hope in her voice. "I really want you to have this. Please, El, it would make me feel better knowing you have this," Destiny said and made the saddest face she could muster.

"Oh, don't do the face. Ugh... fine. I will take it if you stop looking at me like that." Elaine took the book and placed it on her lap. *"I will cherish this more than you know."*

....

After a few quiet moments, Elaine asked, "Did I know her before? You said we always worked better together, so I am just assuming." Elaine squealed in excitement. The thought of actually having a friend who cared for her was exhilarating.

"Yes. The first time you worked together was during the life of Christ. She was named Photini."

"Photini? Who is that?" Elaine wondered with no recognition in her expression.

"The Samaritan woman at the well."

"Oh, I thought that she was a bit of a player. She stayed away from people because she married so many men and then lived with a guy she wasn't even married to. How could she have been a Sure Fire?" Elaine said with disappointment dripping from every word.

"What are you talking about?" Michael retorted. "During that time, women had no rights and were only allowed to live the roles that were assigned to them. She would have never been granted a divorce if she were the one asking for it. She had been abandoned by five husbands, her family, and everyone in that village. She was living with a man who was not her husband because otherwise, she would have been a beggar or died. Everyone saw her as worthless and had outcast her. Christ saw her suffering and offered her grace in place of the condemnation that was offered by everyone else."

Sure Fire | Michaeli Tom

Elaine was left speechless after hearing what Michael had told her.

"She was the first person to believe in Christ as the Messiah who was not of Jewish descent. She ran back to her people, telling them what had just happened to her at the well. You were the first to listen and believe in what she said. Your belief in her words opened the door for others to listen despite their previous dismissal of Photini. Together, you spread the news of salvation to any that would listen."

"That is so sad. She had to be put through all of that suffering. That had to be so lonely," Elaine said while she was lost in her thoughts.

"She had to go through all of her trials so that she could become the woman Jesus needed her to become. Had she not gone through the suffering, her heart-filled testimony wouldn't have had as strong of an impact on the people around her."

"Is that why Lucifer wants to kill me? Because I was the reason for helping others find their way to Jesus and salvation? Is she after all of the Sure Fires?"

Michael turned his head and looked down. "No." His shoulders became extremely tense, and the storm of blue in his eyes was making Elaine nervous. Michael began packing away all of the things they had used for their picnic.

Elaine waited a while for him to finish his answer, but only silence followed. She felt as if she were back on the lake shore once more with a stranger who wouldn't answer her questions. She couldn't stand to not be given an explanation. This is one storm that she would have to face head-on.

"Michael, you said that you would answer my questions. Why does she only want me dead then?"

Michael looked up at Elaine with worry shining in his eyes. "She wants you dead because one of the last souls that you helped… The last of the assignments you took was to reach her soulmate, the cursed one."

"Why would I be the one sent for him?"

"Because… Because I convinced you to help her soul-bond find his way back to God. I had you put into his path because you were the only one strong enough to endure a life with him. I thought maybe if you helped him free his soul from the darkness, maybe you would also be free from needing to go back anymore."

Elaine sat in silence while her heart clenched painfully in her chest. Her throat felt as if it would close completely from the overwhelming emotions that threatened to drown her.

"What was his name?" Elaine forced out angrily. The tension in her body was rising to levels that she was unfortunately accustomed to.

Michael hesitated a moment before uttering one word. "Jeremiah."

One word. That is all that it took to completely knock the remaining air from Elaine's lungs. She had loved Jeremiah dearly despite the innumerable hardships that she had faced to be with him.

"What did you say?" Elaine had tears in her eyes, and her throat was so tight that she thought she would no longer be able to breathe. "Wait, you had said that you never knew where or when I would be sent back. You couldn't have placed me near him."

"It was his last chance at redemption, and I had you come with me to ask for the assignment from the Creator Himself."

"Why would I have asked for such a thing? You certainly couldn't have known that I would help him." Elaine squeaked painfully.

"Of course, I knew that you would help him. It is what you were created to do. You find the lost and broken; then you do everything that you can to lead them to Jesus. You gave everything that you could to those in need, and you always went back because you felt like you still had something to give. Someone else that you could help find salvation through the gospel."

"So, what did you think, huh? That if you worked out how to place me with the one person who could completely drain my soul, I wouldn't want to go back anymore? That I would just stay here? You were supposed to be someone who protected me. Yet, here we find that it was your idea to feed me to the wolves! Not to mention, I have the literal devil trying to find and torture me because I did exactly what you told me to. Great job at this whole guardian angel thing!" Elaine choked out as tears were spilling down her face. Her breathing was getting impossible to catch. "Why did the Creator give me this assignment in the first place? Surely, He had someone else lined out. Why would He give it to me because I asked?"

"No one else was going to take this charge. He had already retired eleven Sure Fires before you, and the rest were too afraid. The Creator never forces His ways onto anyone; it must be by their own choice and free will."

"So, you gambled with my future in order to try and secure his?" Elaine said with hurt evident in her every word. She couldn't believe that the one being charged with her safekeeping would be the one to talk her into such a perilous life.

"You led him from the darkness and helped forge a true relationship with Jesus. You did what no one before you had been able to do. How can you not see how amazing that was?"

"It took me *thirty* years of abuse to do it. Thirty years of being told I was crazy for believing fairy tales. Thirty years of being told I was worthless, pushed around, beaten black and blue. Not to mention that I was having to deal with it all on my own. I couldn't have friends; I didn't even have anyone in my family left. I was completely alone. Had it not been for my relationship with Christ, I don't know what would have happened. He was my rock and the only thing that gave me enough strength to carry on!" Elaine shouted with a glare on her tear-stained face.

Michael stood there facing her with a stoic face, breathing heavily but making no attempt to speak.

"You just watched all of this happen with no cares in the world. For you, once I died, I'd be here with you, and I would have absolutely nothing left to help anyone. I guess you got what you wanted."

"You think that this was easy for me?" Michael retorted.

"You weren't the one living it!" Elaine shouted.

"I was right there the entire time, Elaine! It made my stomach turn every time he even got near to you. I wanted to end his existence for years despite being sworn to protect and aid all of His creation. I felt useless when I was unable to intervene. We accepted this charge, and all I could do was wait until you were alone to sit with you as you prayed. To try and comfort your heart as much as I could after seeing it continuously shattered." The intensity of his voice was ripping out the pieces that were left of Elaine's heart. When she raised her eyes to look into his, she noticed the tears that were falling down his face as well.

"I wanted you with me, yes. I was the one that asked you to do this, but I never meant for everything that happened to occur. He had been changing and getting closer every time. He just needed to see what a true relationship with Christ looked like, and you were the only one strong enough to show him without giving up."

Suddenly, it was as if a light came on in Elaine's mind. "He wasn't human either, was he?" Elaine whispered.

"Elaine…"

"You said that he kept getting closer every time. You called him the cursed one… He lived more than one life. Is he a Sure Fire?"

"He was created to be, but the pull Lucifer had on his soul kept him in a dark and evil place. He should have been leading people to Christ instead of preaching reincarnation and self-idolatry nonsense. I wanted to put a stop to the havoc that he was bringing upon the world, but I was not permitted to intervene."

"You just said how you wanted to end him. If you did, he would have never found Christ, and all my efforts would have been for nothing. You sent me to him for some other reason. Why?"

"I asked you to take the charge to see if it were possible to save him."

"I asked for the reason!" Elaine shouted

"Elaine, you won't understand right now."

"Tell me the truth! Why did you push me to cross paths with someone like him?" Elaine yelled.

"I thought that if he were capable of turning himself around and finding his way back to Christ... I... I thought maybe they all could be saved then, too. Maybe even she could repent and beg forgiveness."

"She... Lucifer? You love her so much that you were willing to trade me for her? You risked my life for a possibility that is never going to happen." Elaine couldn't fight any longer. Now that she was faced with another battle, she found herself totally exhausted.

"He possesses the other half of her soul! If he could find his way back to a fulfilling life in Christ and truly repent for the harm he caused in his existence, she could too. At least, that is what I had hoped. Listen, Elaine, I am sorry. Nothing went to plan, and I... She learned that both you and Destiny were born close to Jeremiah, and she must have known that he was your assignment. She sent so many of her minions to sabotage your lives. She orphaned you both and had you separated as soon as you were together. She poured all of her malice into Jeremiah. You were the only thing that was able to reignite his flame to the point that he was able to overcome his connection with her."

Sure Fire | Michaeli Tom

"Michael! Can you even hear yourself? She hates the Creator and everything that stands by Him. She *hates* all of us!" Elaine stressed.

"Hate isn't the opposite of love. Hate is love that has been wounded. Instead of taking time to heal the wounds, Luce allowed them to fester and rot her heart and mind. Evil was not only allowed but embraced and projected around her to ensure that no matter what, her heart would never heal," Michael said as he wore a stoic face. No longer was there any trace of emotion coming from this being.

"I need some time to myself. I don't want you to talk to me. I don't want you near me. I am going back to the basement, and I do not care where you go. I want it to feel as if I am the only person on this entire planet… or whatever it is! I am leaving right now, and you better not follow me!"

Elaine didn't wait for Michael to respond before she turned and trudged back along the winding path to her safe haven. Her mind was still trying to catch up to all the new information that had just plagued her mind. She had been trying to play mental and emotional catch-up for so long that she was utterly exhausted.

She made her way out of the woods and found the branch to open the door of the safe place. She pulled down on the branch incredibly hard and watched the door spring open. As soon as she made her way down into the basement and to her heaps of pillows, Elaine let everything she had been holding in spill out. She cried and prayed for guidance. She cried until she had no more tears left to cry and prayed until the Holy

Spirit moved and settled her heart. Then she fell into a deep, dreamless sleep.

Chapter 10

memory of a goodbye

Elaine found herself lying in a hospital bed, looking up at the white tile ceiling. She had spent what seemed like so much of her life in hospitals that she was completely at ease in this room (despite the all-white walls and cream-colored tile floors). The lack of color and furnishings gave off a very prisonesque vibe. She had one rather large east-facing window that she was grateful for. It allowed her to watch this morning's sunrise over the mountains and bring to life everything below.

On the bedside table sat a vase of bright yellow flowers. The bouquet included calla lilies, daisies, snapdragons, and her favorite: sunflowers. While looking at the beautiful bouquet, Elaine began to wonder who could have possibly sent her the flowers. She had no one other than Jeremiah, and he would never do something like that.

Before she can look for a card, she is startled out of her thoughts by someone opening the door. Nervously, she looks up to find her husband. Things between them have never been easy, but lately, there has been a sort of shift.

"Why am I in the hospital? How long have I been here, Jeremiah?" Elaine's voice was rough, and her throat burned when she spoke. She could feel no real pain but suspected that she was on some sort of pain pill regimen. Her body felt sluggish and as if it were lagging behind and couldn't catch up to what she wanted to be doing. She needed to know why, so again, she called, "Jeremiah?"

"Three days ago, you fell in the kitchen and hit your head very hard on the countertop and then again on the hardwood floor. I called for the ambulance, and they got there as quickly as they could. They said that you had suffered from a stroke and were unsure if you would ever wake up." Jeremiah's voice cracked, and tears were building in his eyes as he looked at Elaine. He said, "I thought I was never going to see you again or be able to tell you how grateful I am for everything that you have done for me."

Elaine was trying to keep up with everything that Jeremiah was telling her, but it was as if the words themselves were twisting away and being lost from her. The harder she tried to listen to what he had said, the more the room began to spin, and then everything went dark. She slipped away into a dream, a familiar dream that she had whenever the world was too much for her.

When Elaine awoke next, it had to have been evening. The sky was a dark navy color, streaked through with purples and deep reds from the waning sun. She watched as the clouds disappeared and the stars began to shine through the night sky. The whole scene was so peaceful she almost missed the voices in the hall.

"This cannot be right! You are absolutely sure that there is nothing that can be done for her?" It was Jeremiah's voice. She would recognize it anywhere, and she could tell that the news he was getting was that she would not be around for much longer.

"All we can do is try to make her as comfortable as we can until she passes. I am sorry, but there is nothing that we can do. She has a small bleed on her brain, so she can have no blood thinners, but without blood thinners, she will develop clots that may cause another stroke or clog her lungs. There is nothing that can be done. I am truly sorry."

Elaine felt as if she had been punched in the stomach. Tears started free-falling down her face, and her throat was so tight she could hardly breathe. She tried to lose herself to the beauty of the night sky, but the tears were making it impossible to see. The fear of being forgotten began gnawing on her heart.

She heard the door shut, and Jeremiah saw that she was awake and must have heard what the doctor had said. He broke down and sat on Elaine's bed. He grabbed her as tightly as he could, and the two of them sobbed until neither one of them had any tears left to cry.

Elaine's soul had been shattered for the last time, and she truly had no idea how to proceed with anything. She simply lay in her bed staring out at the stars, wishing on every last star that she could see for a miracle. She wished and prayed and prayed and wished until, once more, the darkness enveloped her.

The following morning, Elaine was woken up by the sounds of songbirds singing in the window. Opening her eyes, she looked around to find Jeremiah slumped in the recliner next to the bed, holding his head in his hands. She had never seen him look so lost nor so deep in his own thoughts that he was oblivious to what was happening around him.

She tried clearing her throat to get his attention, but he didn't even budge.

"Hey?" she barely managed to get out above a whisper.

"Elaine! Hey, how are you feeling?" The care she heard in his voice shocked her. She wasn't used to having him care for her, and she had longed for this for so long.

She simply sat on her bed, staring at him as if he had grown another head. Trying to figure out what was behind the sudden change. He asked again with the same gentle tone.

"I feel pretty numb… I just don't know how we got here… Why is this happening to me?"

"Honey, I don't know. All I know is that I am going to be right here for you. Just tell me what you need, and I will do it."

"Why?"

"What do you mean, why?"

Elaine's chest clenched tightly in her chest. All she has ever wanted was for Jeremiah to show her the love she always felt for him, but now it felt off.

"Why are you trying to take care of me now?"

The heartbroken look she saw in his deep, dark brown eyes threatened to swallow her whole. Never has she seen such a look on anyone's face. Knowing that she was the cause of this pain made her wish she had never asked. Yes, he has put her through more pain than she would like to admit, but she never wished to hurt him in return.

"I am sorry, just… never mind." She swallowed down the emotions threatening to spill down her cheeks.

"Listen, I know I have no right to ask your forgiveness. I know I have caused you pain and broken your trust far more than I have been trustworthy. I have taken you for granted and wasted all the time I should have cherished you." He choked on the regret that built up in his heart. Tears slipped down his cheeks as he looked into Elaine's eyes.

Taking a deep breath, he started again. "But I love you! I have loved you from the moment I met you! I am sorry that I waited until now to truly show you how much I truly care for you. Seeing you laying on the floor, surrounded by your own blood. Knowing that you may never open your eyes again. Knowing I may never get to speak to you again or be able to tell you what you mean to me… All I could do was pray for you to be okay… "

Elaine was speechless. She had always imagined him saying those words and longed for him to love her. Now, she was dying. That thought rained down a reality that this would only last a little while.

"I heard what the doctors told you… about me. I woke up, but just for a little while. This isn't going to last, Jer. I don't know what you are wanting from me?"

"I just want to show you that I can be the man you always thought I was."

Elaine's heart felt as if it were bursting.

When the sun started to go down behind the mountains, it was just Elaine and Jeremiah left in the room. Jeremiah walked over to this little speaker and started playing "La Vie en Rose"

Sure Fire | Michaeli Tom 127

by Louis Armstrong. This had always been one of Elaine's favorite songs, and she was very pleased to hear it again.

Jeremiah then sat down beside her and took her hand in his. He studied the look of her hand, kissed her fingers, and then placed her hand on his cheek. They continued to listen to the song in silence, just looking at one another, trying to memorize the features that made up the other half of their lives. Jeremiah's dark brown eyes, black hair that was now sprinkled through with grey, the smile lines around his mouth and eyes growing ever more defined.

The song had ended, and the room was silent. Elaine began to say something, but Jeremiah held up his hand to stop her. She could see the worry behind his eyes, and so she waited patiently for him to say whatever it was that he needed to say.

"Do you remember when we first met? You were eighteen and all on your own. You were headed to your first day of college when those criminals began harassing you. At first, I was just going to walk around the commotion in the ally, but then I saw your face. The first moment I saw you, I knew that I loved you, and I would do anything to meet you."

"Is that why you ran up yelling at them to get away from me? They almost stabbed you before they started running." Elaine interjected.

"I had to get your attention somehow," Jeremiah said with a chuckle. "Once we became friends, I never wanted to lose you. I had to have you in my life, and I was not going to let anyone separate us. We lived in the rent home and went to school together for the next three years, and it was time for us to get real jobs. You were so much smarter than I was, so when I went to mail the applications, I threw all of yours away but one. That way, we would be sure to get work in the same company, and you wouldn't have left me."

"Why are you telling me this?" Elaine asked nervously.

"Because if I had just mailed your applications, your life might have turned out completely differently. You wouldn't have been stuck with me. You wouldn't have had to suffer through my insecurities and jealousy until I finally agreed with you that I needed help. You wouldn't have been hurt, especially not by me, if you would have just been free to go out on your own. For that, I am so incredibly sorry. I am sorry for every time I hurt you. I am sorry for every time you were put in a room like this because I was drinking or strung out. You have no idea how horribly guilty I have felt every day knowing that you should have had a better life than the one I stuck you with."

Elaine had no idea what to say or if she should say anything at all, so she remained quiet.

"I just need you to know that without you… my life would have been an absolute tragedy. I am so sorry that I took out all of my downfalls and frustrations on you. You were the only thing in my life worth living for, and I was a monster. You led me out of the darkness and into a world full of light, love, commitment, and loyalty that I had never known before. You stuck by me for years, even when everyone else told you to run. You stood by me when even I wanted to get far away from me and didn't know how to get away. You found help for me, made me complete my programs, and dragged me to church every Sunday. You are the only person I cared for at all, and I couldn't keep letting you down. You saved my life and my soul, and for that, I am forever grateful."

Elaine reached her right hand up to wipe the tears from Jeremiah's tired face, and when he looked up at her, she was smiling.

"Elaine, Sweetheart, have you heard what I just said? Are you all right, or do you need me to call for a nurse?" There was panic flooding into Jeremiah's voice, and Elaine realized how insane she must seem smiling at such a confession and the memories that came along with it.

"No darling, I am quite fine. I appreciate your apology far more than you could ever imagine, but you must know that I have forgiven you for everything that you had done long ago. Yes, our lives were extremely hard, complicated, and hurtful for the first twenty-three years, but the following almost ten years have been incredibly good to me. The changes that I have seen in you since we were first married have made my life have meaning. Even though you never showed any kindness or love towards me, I could see that you were trying. You just didn't know how to love or be loved by someone. I never lost faith that you would one day be set free."

Elaine wiped more tears from Jeremiah's wrinkled face and pressed a soft kiss to his forehead.

"You may have been the absolute hardest person in the world to live with, but I have always felt that my life was tied to you." Elaine smiled again, and then she said, "But now I can feel my life slipping away. It is the oddest sensation that I can actually feel the time of my life coming to a close."

"Don't say such things," Jeremiah forced his voice to say. His voice was low, and barely any noise was coming out. He said, "I spent far too long being unable to love you because I didn't know how. I didn't know what love even was. By the time I understood love, we had been through so much... I didn't feel worthy of your affection... I pushed you away in case I was incapable of truly loving you. I couldn't handle hurting you anymore. Elaine... I cannot lose you. How am I supposed to stay here without you?"

"I don't want to leave either. My time has come to go home, but you are to stay here as an example to others."

"What example am I to be?" Jeremiah was looking at her like she held all the answers in the world.

Elaine's heart was breaking for Jeremiah. She was forcing her voice to remain steady when she said, "You are to be an example that people can change for the better as long as they have people who love them. You have such a strong testimony, Jer. You need to use it to help others that are hurting. Be the love that you needed from me. Know that I love you, I always have loved you, and I always will love you."

Elaine offered up the best smile she could muster, and Jeremiah kissed her lips.

"And I will always love you to the moon and back. Thank you for giving me the life I always dreamed of. Now sleep, my dear. You can go if you need to. I will be all right. Just know that I will be right here in case you want to stay."

Jeremiah grabbed Elaine's hand and kissed the back of it twice. Elaine smiled as she closed her eyes and felt the darkness surround her, but this darkness was different. It was all-encompassing, and she knew just what that meant. She was dying, but there was no way that she was going to be afraid.

Chapter 11

recognition

When Elaine sat up, she expected to see Michael sleeping in his usual place. She squinted her eyes to try to see through the darkness that enveloped the eerily quiet space.

"Sashiel, Seraphina, Raguel… could you please light the room for me? I need to speak to Michael," Elaine said in a low voice. Her throat was still sore from crying herself to sleep.

Soft light began to fill every inch of the room, just as hope was filling every inch of Elaine's heart. She stood up to face Michael's sleeping form, but there was no trace of him ever coming into the safe place. His bedding remained neatly folded and packed away where Elaine had organized it the night before.

"I want it to feel as if I am the only one left on this entire planet… I want you to go away… Don't you dare follow me… I want it now!"

Those harsh words rang in her mind like a bitter reminder of her past. She had been overwhelmed by all of the information, and instead of working through all of the complications,

Sure Fire | Michaeli Tom 133

she became vicious. She had said the words that she knew would hurt Michael the most, and then she sent him away as if he were the problem. She became cruel to someone who truly loved her.

"I acted no better than Jeremiah," Elaine whispered out.

How easily had it been for her to put all the blame on Michael? How easily had she become cruel? He had shown her his vulnerabilities, and the first time she felt threatened, she twisted the knife in each of his insecurities.

"I need to talk to him!" Elaine said to herself.

Elaine went to the hidden closet and searched through all of the extra supplies to find clean clothes. Luckily, she found a pristine white button-up shirt and a pair of tan pants that looked as if they belonged on the beach. Once she finished getting dressed, she grabbed her survival backpack and headed for the stairs. Elaine began to climb them as quickly as she could, taking as many as three steps at a time. When she reached the top, she said, "Open." To her dismay, nothing happened. She pushed on the dirt wall as hard as she could in an attempt to force her way outside, but it didn't even budge an inch. She yelled, kicked, and punched the doorway until she collapsed on the ground.

She was trapped. Even through her life of solitude on earth, never before had Elaine felt more alone than she did in this moment. Her breaths were coming out fast and uneven. Her heart was clenching painfully in her chest, and her throat felt as if someone were squeezing it shut.

Alone.

Alone. Alone.

I am alone.
Trapped and alone
I will never get out.
Alone. Alone.

Her thoughts were repeating through her mind as if they were blaring through a broken record player that had been set in front of a microphone. The volume was ever increasing along with her despair. No hope of rescue could penetrate the ever faster-revolving cyclone of despair that had taken hold of Elaine's being.

Overcome with defeat, Elaine pushed herself up onto her knees and hung her head low. "Father, please help me. I am sorry for the way that I have been acting. I am sorry for losing sight of what matters most, and that is You. I have been only thinking about myself and allowing fear to rule my actions. I ask that You guide me. I ask for You to show me grace and mercy. Lead me in the way that I am meant to go. Restore my mind and all of my memories. Clean and purify my heart so that I may reflect You and not project my own wounds onto someone else. Mold me into the person that I have always been created to become. Help me do what is right now and forever more. I ask that all of my memories be restored to me and that any locks or barriers that have been put in place be shattered. Lord, I ask that You guide me through the memories and everything that follows. It is through your son's name that I pray. Amen."

As soon as Elaine had finished the prayer for guidance, she felt as if the floor had dropped out from under her. She was falling through some dark space with a small light at the end. As she fell ever closer to the light, she closed her eyes and braced for an impact, but there was nothing. Elaine slowly opened her eyes, but she was now in a place she had never been before.

When Elaine looked around, she realized that she was sitting on a rather large leather sofa in front of a beautiful grand-stone fireplace. A peaceful, warm fire crackled and burned pleasantly in the fireplace, warming the large living space she had found herself in. Beautiful floor-to-ceiling windows framed the wall behind Elaine and allowed her to be bathed by the pale moonlight that flowed gracefully down upon her. Elaine had never felt more at home than she did in this moment. Everything around her felt as if she had designed it herself.

The rich dark wood of the floors, the burgundy lounge chair nestled between the large bookcases. The soft grey rug that complimented the colors of the stones creating the mantle. The pops of yellow in the décor, her favorite color. There was not a single detail about this place that didn't feel welcoming and comforting.

Elaine relaxed into her new environment and let her head fall onto one of the plush yellow throw pillows that adorned the sofa. She let her eyes wander to the large wooden beams that ran the entire length of the room. Each of the seven beams must have been as big around as she was and at least forty feet long. The magnitude of the architecture had captivated Elaine.

As she lay there on the sofa, she inhaled deeply through her nose. The mixture of the cedar smoke from the fire and the beautiful bouquet of wildflowers that sat on the round coffee table next to the sofa relaxed Elaine. This was peace. This is what a home must feel like. Elaine relished the feeling because it had been far too long since she had last felt its ease.

Soft footsteps sounded, signaling that Elaine wasn't alone. Her eyes snapped to the intruder, and she froze. In an instant, it was as if she was now an observer to her circumstance and completely under someone else's control.

Michael patted Elaine's feet and jested, "If you don't move your feet for me to sit down, I am going to have to take all of these delicious snacks with me all the way across the room. You will only be able to smell them."

"Don't you dare." Elaine laughed and raised her legs for Michael to sit. Then she promptly placed her legs over his lap so that she remained lying down.

"Fine, you don't want to sit up. You will just serve as the table then," Michael said as he laid the platter on top of her legs.

The tray held fresh fruits and sweet cream, cheeses, pieces of matzah, and oil. Elaine was most excited for the bowl of vegetable broth that was filling the space with its wondrously aromatic scent. All of the savory foods before her had Elaine's mouth watering. She reached for a slice of cheese when Michael swatted her hand away playfully, saying, "Not even a thank you?"

"Thanks?"

"How rude? You have wounded me, my dearest," Michael said, feigning heartbreak. Elaine thought that he was making the most absurd, sad face that she had ever seen.

Sure Fire | Michaeli Tom

"How could I have even possibly done this to you? My most dearest, most handsomest, wonderfully talented, charming prince of an angel. I am petrified by my mistake. Could you ever see it in your heart to forgive me?" Elaine answered in an even more over-the-top manner. She fluttered her eyes and pouted her lips in order to really sell her act.

Michael heartily laughed at Elaine's exaggerations and said, "I know my acting was bad, but somehow yours was even worse."

"That's only because you didn't have to stare at your face the entire time you were delivering your spiel." Elaine giggled as she started grabbing different items from the tray and eating them.

"Ouch! Now you have a problem with my face as well?"

"No one in existence has ever had an issue with your face," Elaine said with her left eyebrow raised and a smile tugging on the corners of her plump lips.

Michael handed her a spoon and said, "I know of a few mortals that may beg to differ, darling."

"And how exactly did you appear to these mortals? Did you appear as another such mortal, or perhaps you appeared bearing the glory of the Creator carrying a giant sword?"

"Well…"

Loud laughter bubbled up out of Elaine's chest. "You are incorrigible." She laughed for a few more moments before she was once again able to compose herself.

The two continued to talk and laugh as they ate their small dinner. It was as if the two of them agreed on everything, joked about everything, and complimented each other in every aspect of their being. The happiness they found in each other's company was something special.

As the meal drew to a close, Michael drew more into himself. He wasn't as lively as he had been when he had first come into the living space. He was trying to brush off his feelings, but Elaine knew that something was bothering him.

"Are you going to tell me what is bothering you, or are you going to make me draw it out of you?" Elaine said in a determined tone.

"It isn't anything to worry about." Michael deflected.

"We don't hide things from each other. Michael, I go back tomorrow. You can't be upset and not tell me why. Especially not right now." Elaine prodded a bit more.

"I am just worried."

"About what? You have never been worried before. We are a solid team. This isn't going to be any different." Elaine tried to cheer him up.

"This is nothing like before. This time, you are going after the cursed one. He was built to be a Sure Fire as you are, but when his half fell from grace, he had a direct tie to all things evil, dark, and twisted. He has been used as a tool to spread deception and malice by his other half since his very first life. He was used as a puppet to unleash the sin of murder into the world, for goodness sake!"

"I know that he was originally called Cain, and I know who his other half is bound to... Michael... That is why I wanted to ask for this case. He has pulled away from her. Everyone has seen the progress that he has made. He has started to try to do better, but every time he does, she comes in to wreck all of his progress."

"Exactly! Do you think that she is going to let your presence go unnoticed? Do you think that she is just going to let you waltz in and change her soul-bond? She hates us. She hates you because you are tied to me, and she hates me because she feels that I betrayed her. She is going to send every weapon that she has, and they will all be aimed at you! I don't know if I am strong enough…"

Elaine sat up and hugged Michael as tight as she could. She couldn't let him know that she was just as scared as he was. This assignment was completely different than any that had come before. She wasn't just going after a Dark Fire, but the cursed one himself.

"Listen to me, okay?" Elaine pulled back so that she was looking into Michael's stormy blue eyes. She cupped her hands around his face so that she could make sure that he was focused on her. "I know that this life is going to be the hardest thing that we have had to face, but I also know that the Creator is *not* going to abandon us. We are going to have to lean on Him more than we ever have before because He is the only way that we make it out of this successfully. We were created to help the souls that have become lost. We are the beings that the Creator uses to bring the hopeless back to Him. The cursed one isn't necessarily a mortal, but if he can be reached… if he can be turned back to who he was created to be… How many others will follow suit? The Creator is good. He has never left us before, and this time will be no different."

"I can't lose you…" Michael choked out.

"You won't," Elaine said in a sure tone. "I know that everything will work out as it is supposed to. Plus, I have the most qualified guardian ever," Elaine said with a chuckle, but Michael didn't even smile.

"If I were the cursed one, I would be praying to the Creator that He would send His best help, and like it or not, that is us. We were created to protect those weaker than ourselves and find the lost and broken. We were made to lead them back to the only true path back to God. Jesus Christ is the Way, the Truth and the Life. None come to the Father apart from Him. We help him find Yeshua; we did our job." Elaine smiled up at Michael once more. "We mustn't let fear become greater than our love. We are fighting for victory, remember? We just need to remain focused on the Creator and His plans."

"You're right. I will do everything that I can to help you. Just promise me that you will try and be careful!"

"I am always careful!" Elaine stated indignantly.

"I thought we didn't lie to one another?" Michael said with one eyebrow raised.

"I will do my best to be careful, I promise. Plus, you need to remember that hate is not the opposite of love but rather love that has been wounded. We need to show them all that the wounds love can give can be truly healed should they bring all the pain back to Yahweh. He is actual love, not the silly thing mortals have deemed as such."

As soon as the words left her mouth, everything began spinning, and Elaine was lifted up out of the memory she had found herself in. She was then deposited back into her dark little corner of the staircase, staring at the sealed door.

Sure Fire | Michaeli Tom

She sat still for a moment and allowed the memory to wash over her. Soon, a floodgate was opened in her mind, and every single memory from her life was bright and vivid in her mind. Memories of her life here in purgatory, memories of her missions, her friends, her families, and everything that had been missing.

She walked down a dark alley and came face to face with a man who meant her no good. He began to walk toward her until he saw something behind her and ran away as quickly as he could. Now Elaine could see how Michael had made himself appear behind her to ward off the would-be criminal.

The more she analyzed her memories, the more she found Michael. He was never far from her, and he always tried to intervene when the rules would allow, even a few times they did not. Time after time, she saw memories that she thought she was alone, only to find that Michael was right beside her. That he never left her.

Elaine stood up with a renewed determination to find Michael and try to explain everything that had happened. She had to try and make amends. She began pounding her fists on the wall, clawing and kicking at any loose spots.

Suddenly, the floor began to rumble, and the door cracked open. Elaine ran outside as the door finally opened all the way. She ran directly into someone, and they began tumbling down the small path.

Chapter 12

unexpected

"Ohh, my goodness, I am so sorry. I didn't realize that there were still people here. I thought that they had all left weeks ago. Wait. Elaine, is that you?" said an unfamiliar voice.

Elaine looked up to find a short blonde girl standing over her with an outstretched hand. "Who are you?" Elaine asked surprised and a little reluctant to take her hand.

"Me? Ohh, I am Lailah. I was sent as part of the last sweep to make sure that everything has been accounted for," answered the sweet small voice of the new acquaintance.

"Lailah, as in Plato's soul-bond?" Elaine asked.

"Yes, but also Lailah as in one of Elaine's and Michael's best friends... Are you all right, Elaine?" Lailah asked with concern coating her voice.

"You know who I am?" Elaine said a little defensively.

"Sure, I know you. Did you hit your head that hard? Are you going to be okay? I can grab Michael if he's down in the supply room."

"He's not. We got into a fight and I sent him away," Elaine said with a heavy heart.

"But… but you two never argue. What happened out here?" Lailah said as she looked at the scenery around her. "Why are we still standing out here? Let's go inside and get something to drink and snack on and you can tell me everything, all right? Then we can see what we can do to fix whatever happened. It'll be like one of our girls nights," Lailah said with a big smile that reached her beautiful cornflower blue eyes.

Elaine had gotten all of her memories back, and she remembered Lailah. She remembered her as this overly sweet and helpful girl. She was always positive and absolutely wonderful. She had a cropped haircut with bangs that framed her elegant face. She was very thin, but incredibly athletic. When she gave you a hug it sometimes felt as if she were going to crush you with her love.

Elaine had always adored her huge heart and pure innocent spirit. Whenever Elaine was having a hard time preparing for an assignment, Lailah would always be right there to help her feel better and refocus herself. If it hadn't been for Lailah and Destiny, Elaine didn't know where she would have ended up. Her friends gave her strength in times of need.

"I am not sure that there is much left down there for us, but at least it is protected from the elements. It looks like it is going to rain. Those clouds are super dark and low to the ground," Elaine said as she said a mental prayer for Michael's safety.

"Perfect! I hate getting caught in storms. Yuck," chirped Lailah as she led the way into the basement.

Elaine could feel an unease settling around her as she trudged down the steps. She didn't know if it was due to not knowing where Michael was and if he was going to be all right or if she was just not used to being around other people just yet. She just prayed that Michael would be all right and make it back to her safely.

Elaine slowly walked down the stairs. When she reached the bottom step, she shrugged off her survival pack and sat it next to all of Michael's folded-up bedding.

"Girl, I have never seen you this upset. What happened?"

"What hasn't happened?! I died; then, my body was hijacked by the Mistress of Darkness, where I was threatened and chained up. Then, Michael comes to rescue me, but we end up dumped in the middle of a freezing lake, and I almost drown. Then, we find out that I have absolutely no memories apart from my living nightmare of a life with Jeremiah. I didn't know who Michael was. I didn't know who or what I was. I almost killed myself with Jerusalem cherries. We have to run for our lives from stupid hell hounds! Turns out I get panic attacks from large men, and I could hardly stand to be around Michael at all. We finally start talking, and things look like they could work out, but I ask about how I got here, and he takes all of the blame onto himself. He said it was all his idea and that he talked me into it. Yet, when I got my memories back, it was me! I asked for this mission and had to talk him into supporting me! He never wanted me anywhere near Jeremiah. He did it because I asked him to let me take the assignment. Then, even when I didn't remember what actually happened, he still tried to protect me! And I sent him away! I yelled at

Sure Fire | Michaeli Tom   145

him and told him that he did a horrible job as my guardian! Who does that? How can I even look him in the eyes and ask for forgiveness? I was so angry, and I didn't even take a second before I blew up at him. He has protected me this entire time, and I am a horrible human being!" Elaine finished yelling her story with harsh breaths and angry tears filling her eyes.

After a moment of silence, Lailah said, "I thought you weren't a human being?"

"Are you serious, Lai? That is the only thing that stuck out to you? I know that I am a Sure Fire, but I am still a little unsure of the proper English vernacular. I only know the Creator's term for my being," Elaine stated in a huff. "You know, I thought you would be a little bit more helpful or at least supportive," Elaine said with as much disappointment as she could muster.

"Sorry, that was just a lot of information to take in all at once."

"Try having no memories and being stranded with a stranger while the two of you are being hunted down by a psycho!" Elaine shouted in annoyance.

"Okay, I get it. I am sorry, all right?" Lailah said in a gentle and reassuring tone. "Now, one thing that I know for sure is that Michael would never in a billion years leave you by yourself. He has to be around here somewhere. Keep your chin up! He will be back for you, I promise."

"Thank you," Elaine said as she took comfort from her friend's words. It had been so long since she had had an actual friend, and the feeling of friendship was helping to ground Elaine in this moment of uncertainty.

"So… what is your plan from here on?" Lailah said in a dragged-out tone.

"What do you mean?"

"Everyone knows that the gates to this place are going to be permanently shut in just a few days. Are you just going to stay here and wait for Michael? I could take you to the gate with me in the morning if you would like," Lailah said with a large smile plastered on her face.

"There is no way that I am leaving without him. I'm sure that he will come back before we need to leave."

"And if he doesn't… "

"He will! I know he will. I just need to be patient. I need a drink. Would you like some water?" Elaine said, feeling a little flustered. She needed something to do to busy her mind.

"Sure… Do you have anything to eat? I am kind of hungry," Lailah said in a small, unsure voice.

"You don't have to be scared of me. I didn't mean to be rude. I am just a little bit overwhelmed at the moment. Sorry."

"It's okay. You just seem extremely tense."

Elaine pulled out a large pitcher of water, two red apples, a container of berries, and a loaf of bread. She poured two glasses of water and handed one to her friend. Elaine said a small prayer, and the two began eating their meager meal.

"So… you heard all about my crazy story. What have you been up to? I haven't seen you in quite some time! What's new?" Elaine asked, desperate for a distraction from her current situation.

"Oh, you know. I'm just out here doing the Lord's work. Every creature and thing of value has to be removed before

Sure Fire | Michaeli Tom   147

the gates are shut forever. I have been put on this task force to ensure that nothing is left behind. It can seem tedious, but someone has to do it," Lailah said in her beautifully high-pitched voice.

"Well, the Creator couldn't have picked a more detail-oriented person for the job."

"Angel," Lailah corrected.

"Yes, angel. I am sorry. I just got my memories back this afternoon. I am still transitioning out of my human mindset," Elaine said.

"I know that not all of us are archangels like Michael, but we are not people!" Lailah said in a very annoyed tone that Elaine had never heard her use before.

"I said I was sorry. I honestly didn't mean to hurt your feelings… Lai, you know." Elaine was cut off by the sound of the door opening. "Lai, I will be right back to finish this conversation. Let me just talk to Michael really quick. I will be right back!"

Elaine ran to the stairs and took them two by two. She met Michael close to the top of the stairs and wrapped him in the tightest hug that she could muster. Before Michael could say a single word, Elaine was off to the races, speaking as quickly as she could.

"I am so sorry! It was all my idea, and I talked you into this! You have always supported me and taken care of me! You have always had my back and never left my side! How could I have been so crazy to think that you would abandon me?"

"Slow down, Elaine. What are you talking about? I would never abandon you. I had to scout out our quickest path to the gates from here because we leave tomorrow. I wanted it to be as easy as possible because I thought you would still be mad at me."

"I could never be mad at you again! I remember everything!"

"What? How? That is amazing. How much can you remember?"

"I remember everything!" Elaine said through the veil of happy tears.

"Everything?" Michael repeated while he cupped her face in his large hands.

Elaine nodded and stared into those stormy eyes that she adored. Finally, everything in her life felt as if it were going to be all right again. Michael leaned in and kissed her forehead gently as he squeezed her tightly in his warm embrace. Elaine felt so at peace there that she never wanted to move. She could stay there forever, but then she realized that if they didn't make a plan, they actually would live there forever.

Suddenly, Elaine was brought back to reality, and she remembered that she had to tell Michael about their visitor.

"Hey, I have to tell you something else."

"All right, what do you need to tell me?" Michael said with a kind and peaceful smile on his lips. He looked every bit of heavenly perfection and protection that one could imagine. Elaine was fighting hard to keep her focus intact.

"Lailah is here."

"Lailah is what?" Michael said with his smile vanishing.

"She is here. She said that she has been leading up the project to clear out purgatory. To ensure that nothing is left behind…" Elaine's voice kept fading out as she saw Michael's face become more and more worried.

"How long has she been here?" Michael said in a rough tone.

"Maybe twenty minutes. We literally ran into one another. Why are you getting so tense?"

"Where is your backpack?"

"At the bottom of the stairs. Why?"

"You need to grab it as quickly and carefully as you can. Hide behind me because I am not so sure that it is Lailah who is here," Michael whispered.

The two of them made their way down the stairs until they saw Lailah standing behind the large island.

"Hey guys! I was wondering how long it would take you to get over your little argument," Lailah said in a cheerful tone and giggled.

"Hello, Lucifer," Michael said as he stared at the woman standing opposite him.

"Oh, you are no fun anymore. How did you know it was me? She bought this hideous disguise! What gave me away, little brother?" Lucifer jested as she hopped up onto the countertop. Her legs crossed as she sat up in a very rigid position.

"You forget that I know you better than anyone. You can fool a lot of people, but not me. You can never fool me."

"You hear that, Mutt? Seems like your lover boy is still in love with me. Well, I no longer need this disguise. Time to show you what you're missing out on," Lucifer said as a shimmer appeared all around her form. Pitch-black hair started growing from the top of her head and flowed down her back and past

150   *Sure Fire* | Michaeli Tom

her waist. It was thick and beautiful and perfectly straight. She had harshly arched eyebrows that perfectly framed her large bottle-green eyes that shone like stars. She had a light smattering of freckles across her nose and cheeks that were high and proud. Her lips were full and pouty. They were covered in a blood-red lipstick that stood out drastically from her porcelain skin. She looked to be about as tall as Michael. Her tall, imposing frame was only enhanced by her perfect shape.

Elaine's eyes were glued to her as she jumped off the top of the counter and landed ever so gracefully on the floor. Never had Elaine seen such a being. Every single aspect of Lucifer was beyond beautiful. Her face was alluring; her hair was nothing short of perfection; her body was to die for.

Elaine felt a hand grab her upper arm and pull her away from this enchanting creature. Something about her was drawing Elaine in like a moth to a flame, and she hadn't even spoken yet. Dread snaked its way down Elaine's spine as she realized just how much trouble she and Michael had found themselves in.

"Now that is so much better. Don't you agree?" Lucifer said with her perfectly sultry voice.

Elaine felt as if she had been glued to her spot on the floor. Michael had placed himself between Lucifer and Elaine so that she may be protected. For the longest moment, they all stood in silence as they sized each other up. Elaine's mind was running through every possibility that she could foresee, and not one of them seemed to have any sort of good outcome.

"Well, I am just hurt. It doesn't seem as if my dearest friend is happy to see me. Are you all right, dear brother?" Lucifer's tone was sad. If Elaine didn't know better, she would have believed that Lucifer was truly upset.

"Why are you here?" Michael harshly replied.

Laughter bubbled up out of Lucifer's chest, and the musical quality that it contained was enchanting. "Oh, I forgot how funny you were. We should get together more often," Lucifer said with a large smile, showing off her perfect snow-white teeth. "You know exactly why I am here, dear brother. Now that we have both of you together, let's get down to business, shall we?"

"We have no business with the likes of you," snarled Michael in his deep, gruff voice.

Lucifer clicked her tongue three times to express her condescending mood toward Michael's anger. "That is just like you. Ever since the day you kicked all of us out of our homes, you have acted as if you are better than us." Lucifer pouted her lower lip in a frown. Her face pulled the saddest look Elaine had ever seen, but everything about it was fake.

"The fall was entirely your fault. I only did what was right!" Michael shouted.

"You still believe that? How many of us were cast away like trash so that you could play teacher's pet? You helped him dispose of us!" She took a deep breath to recompose herself. "Anyway, that isn't why I am here. You took something that belongs to me. Therefore, I require something of equal or greater value to replace it while it is lost." Elaine's skin crawled at the devil's false, cheerful tone. The evil smile she wore on her face only added a discomforting quality to the eerily calm expression she was portraying.

"You will have nothing," Michael said in a deep and threatening tone.

Lucifer's green eyes shone in excitement. "I love it when you try to fight back. If you won't hand over your little mutt, I will just have to kill you and then take her."

"Don't you dare try to hurt him!" Elaine yelled.

"Hush now, darling; the adults are talking." Lucifer dismissed Elaine's outburst as if it were nothing.

"I already told you that you will have nothing," Michael said again with all the authority he had been granted by the Creator.

Just then, Lucifer grabbed something from the waistband of her black pants and threw it fast as lightning at Elaine. Michael stepped directly in the object's path as it stuck its way deep into his abdomen. His grunt of pain broke Elaine's heart. He bent over for just the slightest moment before he righted himself and pushed Elaine behind himself once more.

"Was that a knife? What is wrong with you?" Elaine shrieked out.

Lucifer's musical laughter was bursting through the room. "Oh my, it is always so comical that you always try to be the hero. Give it a rest, won't you?"

When Elaine looked up at the beast across the room, she saw that Lucifer was holding another knife in her right hand. She knew that Michael would shield her again should the devil try to murder her again, and she didn't know if he would survive. She decided to cry out for help.

Sure Fire | Michaeli Tom

"Father God, we are in need of help. I don't know what to do, but we need to get far away from this place without Lucifer being on our heels. Please do something!" Elaine prayed.

As soon as she finished her prayer, the ground beneath them began to quake and shake so hard that it was almost impossible to remain standing.

"You stay out of this! It has nothing to do with you!" Lucifer shouted at the ceiling while she pointed the knife up.

"Come on! Now!" Elaine shouted as she dragged Michael up the steps.

Each step seemed as if it were harder to climb than the previous step had been. Elaine noticed that it was getting harder due to the fact that she was beginning to have to drag Michael's giant form behind her.

"Please help me! We are almost at the top!" Elaine shouted for Michael to try. She looked down the steps and saw Lucifer at the first step. "Hurry!"

Elaine's determination doubled as she and Michael tumbled out of their hiding place and into the open. As soon as the two were clear of the opening, the ground shuddered and swallowed the opening. The ancient willow that had served as the doorway crashed over the top of the staircase, sealing Lucifer in.

Chapter 13

hopeless

"This won't be able to hold her for long! Elaine, you need to follow the river until it forks; from there, you will need to turn down the path that I marked with white fabric. It will lead you through the mountains and deposit you at the gate. You will need to hurry! Run!" Michael rushed out his orders.

"Let's go then!" Elaine began to walk down the path toward the river.

After only a few steps, she noticed that Michael was not following her. She turned to see Michael facing the fallen willow. His back was tense, and his breathing was harsh. All of his focus was on the spot where the door once had been.

"Come on. We have a long way to go. We need to get started." Elaine tried to gain his attention and pull him from his trance.

"I am not coming. This will not hold her forever. I will stay and buy you the time that you need. Now, go." Michael's deep voice rumbled through the dark forest.

"I won't leave without you."

Sure Fire | Michaeli Tom   155

"Elaine, she found us. It's over! Now I need you to leave. Let me protect you!"

"Not if it costs you your life! I just got all of my memories back, and I can't lose you! So, if you are going to be staying here, so will I!" Elaine shouted as she threw her pack on the ground and sat next to it.

"Don't do this! You need to get going!"

"Not without you! I have made up my mind. Either you can come with me, or we can sit here and wait for your special friend to dig herself out of the tomb she has currently found herself in," Elaine said as she crossed her arms in front of her chest and stared into Michael's eyes with a bored look on her beautiful face.

"You need to reconsider. Please, just go!" Michael pleaded with her.

"No. Thank you for the offer, though."

"Elaine, this isn't a joke. She will get out, and the first thing she will do is come for you. I need you far away from here, and I will just slow you down."

"I am not going to leave you here, and that is final. I have medicine and bandages in my pack. If we can just get far enough away, we can find a place to stop and get you all fixed up. I will take care of you for once! I can do this," Elaine said with all the sincerity she had bubbling up inside her.

"Fine, I will come with you, but if I have to stop, I need you to promise me that you will leave me behind."

"Michael..."

"Promise me!" Michael insisted.

"I promise that if you absolutely can no longer keep up, I will continue to find you help! I will not just leave you!"

"Thank you. Now, please, we must hurry," Michael said as he walked closer to Elaine. He put his hand out to help her up, but when she pulled up, Michael shouted out in pain. Elaine stood to inspect his side when she saw that the knife was still imbedded in his stomach.

"Why haven't you pulled this out? Why is it still stabbing you? We can't leave until we get this taken care of." Elaine was trying her best not to panic.

"Pulling it out could cause far more problems if it isn't taken care of properly. We need to just carry on…"

"Sit still!" Elaine interrupted. "I have bandages right… here. Now, don't move. I am going to remove the knife on the count of three, okay? One… two…" Elaine pulled the knife and pressed the bandage into the wound. She began wrapping Michael's torso with the rest of the bandage and tied it once everything was wrapped tightly.

"There. I know it is still going to hurt, but I will redo everything once we are out of here," Elaine said with a worried smile. She was hoping and praying that her medical care was going to be enough to keep Michael strong enough to make it out of there.

"Thank you, truly," Michael said with love in his eyes. "Follow me. We need to keep up a quick pace. The moons are shining brightly now, but if those clouds roll in, it will be impossible to see. I just hope that it doesn't storm."

Michael and Elaine took off down the path and followed the rough waters of the river. The gentle breeze was picking up and turning into a gusting wind. The distant clouds started showing brilliant flashes of lightning that brought forth enormous rumbles of thunder that continued bouncing back and forth on the canyon walls. The strobe lights and overpowering noise made Elaine feel completely overwhelmed when it was accompanied by the stress of everything else that was currently going on.

"This is the turnoff!" Michael shouted to be heard over the thunder.

The pair were running as fast as they could down this dimly lit dirt trail. The wind was now whipping through the trees above Elaine's head, causing leaves to fly around in little whirlwind patterns. Elaine felt as if she couldn't see anything over a few feet in front of her face. The dark skies were quickly becoming darker; sinister clouds were rolling in faster than Elaine could run. A fact that was deeply disturbing to Elaine due to her current ability to outrun Michael.

Elaine abruptly stopped running and began looking up and down the sides of the mountains that were currently surrounding her. She had to find a safe place for them to rest. If she didn't find one soon, she couldn't even bring herself to imagine what would happen if she wasn't able to find somewhere for them to be sheltered from the storm that was quickly outpacing them.

"What are you doing?" Michael shouted. "We need to keep moving!"

"I know, but we need to be moving up! When this rain hits, it is going to flood this entire valley. If we are still down here, we are going to get washed away! We need to find shelter!" Elaine continued searching the different features on the mountainsides. "We need to find... a cave! Follow me!" Elaine excitedly shouted.

Elaine began to climb up the rocky face of the mountain to her left. The surface of the rocks was smooth; Elaine began to worry that if they weren't able to reach the ledge before the rain reached them, the rocks would be far too slippery to climb. She doubled her efforts to scale the rock wall as quickly as she could. She climbed the final ten feet faster than she ever thought that she could.

Michael was following at a much slower pace. The wound in his side had started to bleed through the bandaging that Elaine had placed on him. His breathing was hard, and even though he tried to keep his pain unnoticeable, Elaine knew that it must be excruciating. She knew that she needed to find a way to help him climb faster so that he could get the treatment that he desperately needed.

Elaine hurried into the cave and dumped her survival pack out on the ground. "Raguel, I could really use some light right about now!" Immediately, bright beams poured from the celestial light that filled the entire cave. Elaine found the bundle of rope and began unwinding it so that she could lower the rope to Michael. As soon as the rope looked long enough to reach him, Elaine tossed the loose end and called out, "Michael, take the rope!"

Elaine wrapped the end she still had around her waist and braced herself against a large boulder that was situated close to the edge of the platform. She felt Michael tug on the rope just as the first raindrop brushed her cheek. "Hurry!" Elaine pleaded.

Michael gripped the rope and began to climb a little easier. He was making the ascent at a decent pace. Then, out of nowhere, it was as if someone flipped a switch, and the rain began to pour. Sheets of raindrops flowed down upon the exposed duo, making Elaine pray for Michael to be able to reach the top safely.

Michael's foot slipped, and he crashed into the side of the mountain. He pulled on the rope as it was his only lifeline as he dangled thirty-five feet above the valley below. The rope squeezed Elaine's waist painfully as she tried to keep it from unwinding. She used all of her strength to hold steady. The boulder helped Elaine wedge herself into an immovable position.

After what felt like an eternity in the freezing rain, Michael reached the top. Elaine was able to unwind the rope from her waist and take two steps toward him when he collapsed.

"Michael! Michael, get up!" Elaine cried. Tears now flowed down her cheeks just as quickly as the raindrops.

"Michael, please! I am begging you!" Elaine whimpered.

Elaine grabbed Michael's arms and began dragging his incredibly heavy form toward the entrance of the cave. Each step had Elaine's tired muscles screaming out in protest.

"Only a few more steps. I have medicine, bandages… ugh… I have food and blankets. Just hang on a little longer!"

Elaine struggled to pull Michael far enough into the cave that he was no longer being pelted with rain. She hurried to the scattered supplies to find the flask of medicine and new bandages for Michael's wounds. She grabbed Raguel and hurried to Michael's side so that she could begin working on changing out his bandages. She pulled off the blood-soaked bandage and exposed the wound. Her fingers worked diligently and efficiently on cleaning the wound before she treated the area and rewrapped it. Then she checked Michael's pulse and found that it was fading. He must have lost too much blood.

She grabbed the flask of medicine and forced a couple of gulps down his throat. Michael remained motionless. His shallow breathing was tearing Elaine's heart to pieces. She rolled a sheet up, placed it under his head, and unfolded another to cover him.

"Please wake up..." Elaine sniffled.

She was exhausted, but sleep was the furthest thing from her mind. She sat next to Michael and wrapped her arms around her knees with her chin resting on her knees. Her eyes remained glued to Michael's chest because as long as it was rising and falling, Elaine knew that he was alive.

Once his breathing seemed to even out, Elaine started to monitor the storm that continued to rage outside. Lightning continued to flash its brilliant light outside the cave's entrance, but the sound of the thunder had been slightly muffled. The harsh pitter-patter of the raindrops at the cave's mouth was a constant racket that Elaine was desperately trying to tune out.

Sitting in the cave of constant noise, but without being able to talk to Michael, made Elaine feel as if she were going to go insane. There was no way for her to know how much time had passed. The only thing she could do at the moment was wait for Michael to wake, for the rain to stop, or for the sun to come up. Elaine felt as if she had been alone in that cave for hours, but there was still no change in Michael's or the sky's conditions.

"I can't take the silence anymore," Elaine said as she stared out of the mouth of the cave, watching the raindrops continue to fall in a torrent upon the rocky mountainside.

Elaine stood up and walked over to her empty pack and began to organize the supplies that had been strewn about all over the floor. She picked up the flask of water and two cans of various snacks to enjoy once everything had been tidied. Elaine had always found solace in cleaning; something about the freshly wiped surfaces, neatly folded laundry, and crisp aromas from the different cleaning supplies and oils always put her at ease.

Here in the cave, she was able to neatly fold up all of the extra linens, set out each container in an organized and easy-to-find manner, and then gather the knives that she had packed in case of danger. She set her empty pack behind everything where it could lean on the wall without falling over. She thought that if she needed to pack everything up in a hurry, everything needed to be placed in the order that it must be packed up, including the pack itself.

Once she was happy with the order of her possessions, she grabbed her snacks and water and returned to the area where Michael was resting. She took a few gulps of water only to realize how parched she had truly been. She knew that she couldn't finish off the water or she would make herself sick, not only that, but then she would have nothing to offer Michael when he woke up.

If she had anything larger, she would have set it out in the rain to try to collect as much as she could, but currently, every container was holding something precious. There had to be something that she could use. Elaine knew that this one flask would never be enough water for the both of them. Especially when she considered how incredibly thirsty she was from their little getaway. Michael must be even more depleted due to the injury he sustained while trying to protect her.

Elaine decided to stack all of the food onto one of the sheets so that she could use the two medium-sized containers to collect water for them to drink. "Something has to be better than nothing, right?" she thought out loud. She placed one of the sheets close to Michael's head and proceeded to dump both of the food containers out onto the center of the cloth. Then she took them and walked to the mouth of the cave. There, she noticed that the winds had calmed down, but the rain remained steady. She ran out onto the ledge and placed each container in a spot where she hoped that they would be able to stay upright.

Running back into her sanctuary, Elaine found herself once again drenched from head to toe. She walked to her stash of sheets and flung one around her shoulders as if it were a very large towel. She returned once more to Michael's side and sat down so that she could check his vitals.

Michael's breathing remained steady, and if Elaine's reading was correct, his pulse was becoming stronger as well. She desperately hoped that his pulse was actually gaining strength and she wasn't allowing her wishes to influence her counting. She wanted so badly for Michael to open his eyes.

"I know that you made me promise that I would leave, but I can't," Elaine whispered. "I finally know who I am, and a large part of that is due to who you are. I finally had caught up to the reality of everything that we are, and I was desperate to find you so that I could apologize for everything that I had said." Elaine sniffled.

A brilliant flash of lightning luminated the entire cave, and the clap of thunder shook through Elaine's chest. She expectantly looked toward Michael, but he remained still. Elaine's heart broke, and she began to sob. If something as powerful as that couldn't rouse Michael from his slumber, maybe everything that she did was too little too late.

Elaine tried her best to gather her thoughts. If this was going to be the last time that she was able to speak to Michael, she wasn't going to waste it.

"Michael… I don't know if you can hear me, but I have so much that I need to tell you! Ugh, keep it together. Okay." Elaine took a deep breath before she was able to continue. "When I was trapped in the cellar, I… I had quite a lot of time to think back on everything that we had been through. I was so mad at our circumstances. I was mad at myself for not being able to get out of this insane situation. I was mad at you for seeming to be the only one who knew what was going on. And you, you just let me be mad at you even when you were taking the blame for my placement with Jeremiah. Why would you do that?"

Elaine hugged the sheet tighter around her shoulders as she looked out of the mouth of the cave. The storm that had been raging outside had calmed to a slow, steady fall of rain.

The soft pitter-patter of the raindrops was a drastic contrast to the torrent of thoughts and emotions that were raining down on Elaine's mind.

How did everything go so wrong?

Why was all of this happening?

Why couldn't everything have just gone to plan?

The thoughts continued to build and overwhelm all of Elaine's senses until she felt defeated. Tears were building up in her eyes as she desperately wished she could quiet her mind. Tears of anger, tears of sadness, and tears of disappointment in herself wanted to rush down her face like a furious waterfall of sorrows. It was as if the depth of her despair knew no bounds as it continued to spiral downward.

Her breathing was becoming labored as the beats of her heart quickened in her chest. Panic was settling in and painfully squeezing her throat. Elaine had become overwhelmed to the point of a full-blown panic attack. She felt as if she were drowning, and there was no one there that would be able to pull her out.

Suddenly, the story of Peter walking on water flooded into her mind. He had focused on the large waves around him, on the worries of the world, to the point that he was swallowed up by the waves. It was only when he turned his attention back to Jesus that the Lord was able to help him up and out of the water. Elaine realized that her focus had been torn from her created purpose, and now she was engulfed by the worries of her situation. She was trying so hard to accomplish everything on her own that she forgot that she had never been alone.

She closed her eyes as she prayed. She poured her heart and soul into her prayer. She asked why everything was turning out the way that it had been. She told Him how she was feeling truly abandoned and forgotten. She asked for help and guidance: where her next move was supposed to be and when it should be done. Most of all, she cried and unleashed every emotion that she had bottled up from her mortal life to this very moment. She hid nothing from the Creator, and by the time she was finished praying, she felt as if the weight of the entire world had been lifted off of her shoulders.

Elaine sat in silence for just a little while longer, staring at the mouth of the cave. The soft rain had eased a little more to just a light smattering of sprinkling raindrops. The fresh scent of the forest after a good rain was wafting into the cave, carried by the gentle breeze that was tugging on Elaine's long hair.

Elaine stood up and walked outside to see if the two containers had collected much water. She was pleased to find them both filled to the very top. Carefully, she carried them back into the cave, where their lids sat next to Michael. She placed the first lid on the larger jar to make sure that she didn't spill any of the water. When she went to grab the lid for the second jar, she noticed a beautiful pair of blue eyes was watching her.

"Michael! You're awake!" Elaine yelled as she leaped up to hug him. He grunted as if she had punched him, and she remembered the wound that he had sustained and quickly apologized.

"I am so sorry! I have been losing my mind in this cave," Elaine said as a blush sprung up to her cheeks.

Michael tried to say something and coughed.

"Here. Drink this. I just collected it from the rain," Elaine said as she handed him the still uncovered jar of water.

Michael gulped down the refreshing liquid as if he were going to die of thirst at any moment. Elaine sat quietly and watched him, waiting for any sign that he would need anything else.

"How long have we been here?" Michael's gruff voice said.

"I am not sure. I don't know how to tell time here, and it has been storming since you collapsed. It has just now eased up, but the rain hasn't stopped completely yet."

"I thought you promised that you would leave?"

"It was storming outside. I couldn't go anywhere even if I did know where I was going. Like it or not, you're stuck with me," Elaine said with a cheeky grin.

Michael slowly pushed to a sitting position and surveyed the cave. "How did you get me in here?"

"Well, it wasn't easy. You are much heavier than you look," Elaine said with a small chuckle. "I knew that it had to be done, so I did it. I almost went crazy not knowing if you were going to be all right. I second-guessed everything that I did. I was praying and hoping that you were going to be okay." Elaine was cut off by the emotions clogging her throat.

"Look at me," Michael said, but Elaine continued to look at her hands that were folded in her lap. "Look at me. Look here," Michael said as he lifted her chin. "I am alive because of you. I am here. Everything is going to be all right."

Elaine had not trusted anyone in such a very long time, but when Michael told her something, it was as if it were set in stone. She trusted him as much as she trusted in herself. If

Michael said that everything was going to be okay, then Elaine had nothing to worry about.

"I know you are probably tired, but we need to get to the gates. Are you ready to go home?"

Home. One word that had such a deep impact on Elaine's heart. She had longed for a home for her entire life, and now she was so close to getting there. The trepidation of uncertainty was far outweighed by the sheer excitement of being in a place where she truly belonged.

"I thought you'd never ask," Elaine said teasingly with a genuine smile. She was going home, and nothing was going to stand in her way.

Chapter 14

one way home

Elaine was finally able to breathe freely. All that was left for her to do was hike to the gates and begin her life in the place that she was always meant to be. She and Michael packed the supplies back into her survival pack once Michael had another dose of medicine and had his bandages changed out. The wound was almost completely healed, but neither of them wanted to risk infection or having it reopen due to their journey.

They decided to leave a jug of water and their food supplies out of the pack so that they could eat and drink as they walked. They had no time to waste sitting still to have a meal despite both of them being absolutely ravenous. Elaine fashioned a sort of pouch out of one of the sheets so that the food could be easily grabbed from her side. Michael now wore the survival pack on his back, one knife sheathed to his belt and another tucked into his boot.

"I would not want to make you angry," Elaine said in an attempt to lighten the mood.

"I doubt many people would. You don't have to worry about that, though. When I said that I would never hurt you, I meant that with every fiber of my being."

"I know you did. You went as far as to take the blame for my actions. I still don't understand why you did that."

"What good would it have done to tell someone who has no memories that the chaos around them was from a decision that they don't remember making in the first place? It would have seemed more like a lie than if I just took the blame. I could not risk losing the small amount of trust that we had just started to build. People move on from anger faster than they do from having their trust broken. I was just hoping that we would have had more time or that you would regain your memories and fall madly in love with me once again," Michael said with a wink and a smile.

"You are incorrigible." Elaine laughed.

"Yes, but you love me, so it doesn't matter. Now, are we ready to see what we are dealing with?" Michael said as he began to walk to the ledge to overlook the valley. They needed to find the quickest way to the gate, but the rain had flooded the bottom of the valley, and some trees had been knocked over certain pathways.

"My initial thought was to follow along the bottom of the valley, but that has been overruled by the Creator. The path along the far side of the foothills seems to have had a mudslide sometime in the night, so that one is out as well. The only path that can get us out of here is if we follow along this rim of the mountain. It'll keep us out of the marshlands below, and we won't have to worry about getting bogged down in the mudslide. The trick with this path is that it seems to get rather narrow just before we are cleared to descend."

"I grew up in the mountains of Colorado. If you are worried about me, know that I will be just fine," Elaine said with a proud smile on her face.

"Well then, I guess it is settled. Let's get going." Michael retorted.

The two began walking side by side along the rocky ledge that seemed to have been cut out of the side of this enormous mountain. The ledge had a slight rise to the path, forcing them to climb higher up the mountain rather than staying at a consistent level. Michael pulled Elaine to the inside of the path so that he could walk next to the ever-increasing drop-off.

"How chivalrous of you." Elaine jested. "But honestly, thank you. It was getting a bit nerve-wracking seeing how far up the mountain we are without any sort of safety equipment."

Nervously, Elaine grabbed a handful of their makeshift trail mix and began snacking as she walked.

"Are you not going to share?"

"Oh, do you want some?" Elaine said as she shifted the pouch from her right hip over to her left so that Michael would be able to get some food as well.

"I would love some, thank you," Michael said as he began eating some cashews and almonds.

Handful after handful was shoveled into his mouth, to the point Elaine began to worry that he would choke.

"Slow down. You are acting as if you think it is going to run away. Here, take a drink so that you don't choke. I don't think this is a very safe place to have to perform the Heimlich maneuver," Elaine said as she held out the jar of water that was strapped to her side.

Elaine giggled at Michael as he grunted in agreement and took the drink from Elaine. She thought he looked just like a little kid who was far too impatient to simply eat the food they were given in a correct manner. Instead, they shove all of the food into their mouths to prove that they had eaten everything that they were supposed to so that they could hurry up and go play.

Once Michael had cleared his mouth and had a few drinks of the water, he pointed up toward the third peak that was along the mountain range they had found themselves hiking along.

"You see that peak right there?" Michael nodded toward the top of the third mountain and continued pointing.

"The big one?"

"The gate is on the back side of that mountain. We are keeping a pretty even pace, but we need to make sure that we get through those gates today. They are scheduled to close permanently this evening. The Creator is setting everything into motion for the final battle. The war in the spiritual realms has been raging for a while, but it is almost time for everything to be reconciled back to Him."

"Are you talking about the second coming? Jesus is going back?" Elaine said with a jolt of shock running through her body.

"Yes, that is why it was imperative that Jeremiah be saved in this life. It was the last time any soul would be brought into the world. If he didn't find his way back to the Creator in this life, he would have been lost forever."

"Is that why I was so determined to take his assignment?" Elaine uttered in a small voice.

Michael only looked ahead and sighed.

"He is half of her, you know. Somewhere deep down, maybe she could change... " Elaine tried to give Michael hope that, somehow, even Lucifer could still be saved.

"How I wish that were true. She used to be the most dependable... it was long ago."

"That doesn't mean you love her any less. People hurt others, angels have hurt others; the only perfect being is the Creator. Only He can restore that which is broken. None are too far gone for Him to redeem them."

"But they must first ask. Then, they must turn from their ways once they do ask. I don't see that happening when it comes to Luce," Michael said as he grabbed a giant red rock and used it to pull himself up onto a higher ledge. "Here, take my hand, and I will lift you up."

"This ledge looks far more narrow than the one we were on," Elaine said as she tried to keep herself from looking over the steep drop to her side.

"It is, but the one we were on hits a dead end up there. See?" Michael pointed to a steep wall that would have been in their way further along their previous path.

Elaine could clearly see the abrupt stop from their new pathway. "Well, it is a good thing you saw that, or we would have had to backtrack," Elaine said as she began following behind Michael. This new path was far steeper than the previ-

Sure Fire | Michaeli Tom 173

ous, and Elaine was doing everything she could to try and hug the inside wall so that she wouldn't tumble off the side.

"I didn't see it. I told you I know this place. We will follow this all the way to the middle of that mountain there. Do you see how it snakes up and around the way and then begins to dip low into the side of the next mountain?"

Elaine followed Michael's finger as he spoke so that she could see the routes they would be taking clearly. "Yes, I see it, but it looks too steep to walk down over there." Elaine was looking at the angle of the path and beginning to worry that she wouldn't be able to complete this hike at all.

"It is, but it forks up just a tick right there. Do you see that?"

"No. All I see is a bunch of boulders and that one path."

"Oh, you are still looking too far down the way. It forks right here. Then it begins to wind around the side of the mountain in a large *C* shape," Michael said as he traced the small trail with his finger for Elaine to follow.

"Okay. And that will lead us to the other side of the mountain. How do we get to the gate?"

Michael laughed out loud. "Let's focus on getting through this stretch of wilderness first. Once we are off the rocky side of the mountain, we will find a thick forest. It will have its own set of challenges to navigate, especially after that heavy rain. Be praying that there weren't any mudslides," Michael said as the tension in his shoulders told Elaine how dangerous this little excursion would truly be.

Step by step, they worked their way along the rocky edges of the mountains. It reminded Elaine of the steep cliffs and mountain walls of the Grand Canyon. The red rock was marbled through with black, brown, and tan stone. It was beautiful, but the rustling rubble under her feet kept her on edge. She was wishing for this path to end so that they would be far from these harsh cliffs and under the protection of the trees once again. She would trudge uphill in the mud happily if it meant that she would be free from a deadly freefall.

The butterflies that were swarming around in a frenzy inside Elaine's stomach were doing nothing to help her stay focused. Heights had never bothered her all that much before. She normally would classify herself as an adrenaline junkie, but the swirling torrent of fear was throwing off every step she took. She was stumbling and unable to truly focus on completing this hike in any sort of graceful manner, but she wasn't even sure she was worrying about herself.

When she looked at Michael's form just in front of her, she noticed that he was still very sluggish and flinching every time a step forced him to stretch out too far. Elaine knew that if Michael were to stumble here on this narrow overhang, she would have no possible way to help him back up. If he were to overwork himself without being fully healed, Elaine would be stranded here on the rocky face of the mountain.

"Hey, would you like to take a short break? We could get a drink and catch our breath." Elaine suggested.

"Are you getting tired?" Michael asked as he tried to peek behind his shoulder. As soon as his focus was no longer on the path, he stumbled. Small rocks scattered down the sheer cliff side as his left foot seemed to shift out from under Michael's body. Elaine's heart seemed to stop until Michael caught his balance once more.

"Oh, good grief, Michael! It felt like my soul was trying to leave my body!" Elaine huffed. "I am not tired, but I didn't want you to overexert yourself so soon after being injured. I was trying to be thoughtful, not distract you so that you fell!" Elaine said as one hand clung to the side of the mountain, and the other was trying to make sure her heart stayed inside her chest.

"I can't help it if there are loose rocks on the pathway. I am going to be fine, so just try to take a few deep breaths."

"I swear if you tell me to calm down, I may push you over myself."

"Look, we have almost made it to the fork. If you look over my right shoulder, you will be able to see the ledge that we need to climb is only about fifty yards ahead of us. If we can make it there quickly, we can sit down for a while to eat and relax. The gate is only a short distance from there."

"Fine, but you better not trip again. With the way my heart is beating, I may pass out if you do that again."

"I will try my hardest. I hardly can control the composition of the walkway. It isn't even a created path, but the Father has blessed us with a way to get us home."

"Why did He put us here?" Elaine asked the question that had been plaguing her mind from the moment she arrived in this strange landscape.

"I honestly don't know. He must have a plan of some sort, but I was not informed. Watch your step right here. There is a split in the rock that could easily roll your ankle."

176   *Sure Fire* | Michaeli Tom

Michael and Elaine continued making their way along the slender and unreliable trail. The space that they were walking had narrowed so much that each step was a gamble with their very lives by the time they were able to crawl up onto the landing of the new trail.

Elaine's nerves were frazzled beyond anything that she would have expected when she got ready to set out on this journey. All she wanted was a bit of time to relax and decompress from everything that she had been going through. Nothing had been right. Nothing had gone to plan. All she ever wanted to do was help find those that were lost and help point them back home. Yet, now she feels as if she is the one that is lost. Only now, there is no one coming to point the way.

"What is running through your head? I can see the wheels turning from here," Michael said as he fixed them a place to sit down.

"It's nothing."

"It is never nothing. What is wrong?"

"What is wrong?" Elaine huffed. "Everything is wrong! I have spent my entire existence helping others, risking my neck for them, and giving everything that I have for them to have a better life. Now, after doing what I was supposed to, I find myself needing help and finding absolutely no one around! What did I do wrong? Why is this happening to me?"

"Are you done?"

"What do you mean? You are being insensitive!"

"The Creator could have let Luce have you. But He sent me! I have been here with you the *entire* time. I have been trying everything I can to help you! I have told you that I don't

Sure Fire | Michaeli Tom 177

know what is in the works, but He has never once left us! He isn't going to start now," Michael said with a hint of hurt in his controlled voice.

"I didn't mean that you weren't helping…"

"You have been focused on you this entire time. If you would look around, you would find far more good than bad. He has provided everything that we have needed without fault, and He has done incredible things when we can no longer help ourselves. We should be thankful that He has a wonderful plan and that He chose to use us! He could have picked absolutely anyone, but He chose us, Elaine. It is our job to put in the work to accomplish the task at hand."

Michael began to eat as he stared at the rocks beneath his feet. Elaine had been so taken aback that she wasn't sure how to respond. He had chosen her for whatever this was, and she was so focused on her own understanding that she was missing the truth that was around her. He had made sure that every single event of the last few days hit at the correct time. Michael found her immediately after she ate the poisonous berries. They made it to the shelter in the nick of time before the door would have been lost. They had plenty of food and water. They got into a fight so that Michael would not be there when Lucifer arrived. He buried her under the old willow so that they were able to escape. He sent the typhoon to wash away any trace of their route and allowed Michael to heal.

It was as if an electrical current ran through Elaine's entire body as the realization set in that He had not abandoned her for a single moment. He had taken care of the both of them, even when things were looking the most foreboding and abysmal. The Creator had cared for both of them, and He had never forgotten them for a moment in all of their existence. His love for them was never-ending.

After a moment of Elaine being lost in her memories of every time the Creator had saved her, she wanted to talk to Michael. She looked up to see if she could find the words to say to him, but all she found were dark, heavy rain clouds. The blue skies that had been gracing them as they hiked had been quickly replaced by these thick storm clouds.

"Um, Michael. I think we had better start moving now. If it starts raining like it did yesterday, we may not even make it a short distance before we are thrown off a waterfall," Elaine whispered in trepidation.

"Something isn't right. When did you begin to feel abandoned?" Michael asked with a very stern face.

"I don't know… I guess right about the time you asked me what was wrong. Why?" Elaine tried her best to keep her voice calm despite the panic that was building in her chest.

"She has escaped. We need to hurry to the gates," Michael said in a very deep, authoritative voice. He left absolutely no room for arguments. "We need to move. Now!"

Elaine grabbed the pack that Michael had set on the ground beside her and began racing up the path behind Michael. She wasn't sure what was going on, but she knew she needed to be ready for absolutely anything to happen. The only things that she knew for certain were that Michael was going to help her and that the Creator would never abandon them. For if God was with them, who then could stand against them? This would be the verse that she would draw strength from until she was able to stand face-to-face with the Creator. Until that time came, she was going to give everything she had in order to keep herself and Michael alive.

Chapter 15

At Last

Michael and Elaine had been sprinting through the wilderness in an attempt to reach the gates of heaven before any more misfortune would be able to befall them. They were able to run along the pebbled path that led them to the far side of the mountain. There, it opened up to a hidden ecosystem full of tropical trees, flowers, and vines that snaked through almost every living thing. It was as if the vines were serving as the circulatory system of this humid jungle, connecting everything as one.

Elaine leaped over a fallen tree that was being consumed by bright blue mushrooms. When she landed on the other side, her feet sank deep into the thick black mud. The suction from the mud had her cemented in place.

"Michael!" Elaine shouted to get his attention.

"Yes?"

"I can't move! My shoes are stuck, and I have nothing to pull them out."

"We are almost there. Just take your shoes off. Your feet won't get stuck."

Elaine's shocked face told Michael that she did not agree with his plan. "Are you serious?"

"Elaine, we don't have time. If I pull you out, you will more than likely lose one or both shoes anyway. We don't need them, but we do need to get moving. Please." Michael finished in an exhausted tone.

"Fine! But you are replacing these with something cute once we get out of here!" Elaine huffed.

Elaine quickly unlaced the boots that she had been wearing and began pulling her feet out of them. The ironlike vise that the mud had placed on the shoes didn't even allow them to budge when she freed herself from them. Squishing her feet into the sludgy muck was not on her list of things she enjoyed, but now she was free to begin racing through the jungle.

Following Michael as they wove through trees, under vines, over small streams, and between walls of vegetation, Elaine was growing hopeful for their escape.

"It is right there," Michael yelled in an elated voice.

Elaine looked past his left shoulder to see this large woven arch. The wood looked like a sort of bleached knotted pine. It was so pale that it was almost pure white, with large tan spirals flowing through the wooden beams. The arch rested upon a large white marble platform that was raised three steps from the ground level. It must have been around thirty feet across, and the peak of the arch must have been raised fifty feet into the air. This structure was massive and immaculate.

The thing that struck Elaine the most was that between the pillars, the view was not that of a jungle. When she looked at the scene before her, she saw fields of green grass that had white flowers sprinkled throughout. The soft rolling hills made the fields look like an ocean of foliage. The bright blue sky in the arch contrasted drastically with the near-black clouds that were covering Michael and Elaine.

Elaine felt as if the landscape itself was calling out for Elaine to come home. It was pulling her faster toward the sanctuary that the grassy fields offered to her. Elaine's heart was beating wildly in her chest as the pair neared the first step of the arch.

As soon as her foot touched the first stone, the entire platform exploded into the most radiant light Elaine had ever witnessed. Pure white light exploded like a beacon in the night sky. They were finally home. All they had to do was cross over the threshold.

Suddenly, Elaine felt a hand clamp down on her shoulder. It ripped her back with such force that she was sent flying into a large royal poinciana tree. The force with which she hit the tree had showers of its red flowers softly raining to the ground. Elaine couldn't breathe for a moment and simply lay on the ground gasping for air. Her lungs felt as if they might implode at any moment.

As she lay trying to catch her breath, she heard a crash, then another, then another. She caught her breath enough for her to lift her head. It took her a moment to find where the noises were coming from, but when she did, she saw Lucifer throwing Michael like a rag doll. He spun through the air and landed in an unnatural position at Elaine's feet.

Elaine rushed to his side and began assessing his wounds. She took off her pack and began getting out medicines and bandages. Michael was able to take a few gulps of the tonic before Elaine heard the sound of leaves crunching to her right. She pulled her knife and placed herself between Michael and this monster.

Elaine was surprised to see Lucifer like this. Her long, perfect hair was matted together with twigs and leaves scattered throughout. Her face and hands were covered in mud. Her nose was bleeding, as was a long scratch across her left cheek. Her glass green eyes that had been so dazzling just the day before were now void of color. Deep black pools of evil now stared back at her.

"Why are you doing this? All we want to do is help you! We wanted our friend back!" Elaine shouted at the beast as she inched ever closer.

Wicked laughter bubbled up and out of this creature. Haunting and echoing off the surroundings as an ominous warning. Lucifer smiled a dark, deranged smile that sent shivers down Elaine's spine.

"You think you could help me? You're nothing! You're a mistake that needs to be corrected. All of you mortals are!" Lucifer's voice was harsh and cutting.

"You were meant for so much more than this. Remember who you are!" Elaine pleaded.

"I am the most powerful being on earth and beyond! That is who I am!" Lucifer spat. "Now, all I must do is dispose of you and the Creator's little pet, and I will be unstoppable," she said with another horrifying smile.

Lucifer picked Elaine up by her throat and was about to speak when a loud burst of thunder rolled through the valley.

The very ground they were standing upon was trembling as if it were afraid.

"Enough!" a calm voice called from behind Elaine.

Lucifer dropped Elaine and scurried back from everyone.

"Stop," the voice said once more.

Immediately, Lucifer stopped in her tracks and fell to one knee. Elaine turned to find the kindest pair of brown eyes watching her with complete love.

"Yeshua?"

"It is nice to see you again, Elaine."

Having heard Him say her name, she rushed to Him and started babbling about everything that had been going on. She needed to tell Him everything that had happened. She wanted to ask Him why everything was falling apart. So many thoughts were racing through her mind.

"I know. Everything is all right." The sincerity in His voice calmed every nerve in Elaine's body. She trusted that she would be taken care of as long as she remained by His side. Suddenly, Elaine's thoughts cleared, and she remembered that Michael was lying in the dirt behind her.

"Please, help him," Elaine asked in such a small voice.

"Michael, be healed." The gentle voice of Yeshua washed over Michael's body and repaired every malady afflicted upon him. Even the scar that he had worn on his shoulder was completely healed.

"Thank You, Sire," Michael said as he rose to a kneeling position with his head bowed.

"Now, if you both will excuse me. I have someone I need to have a word with," He said as He walked toward the place where Lucifer knelt.

"What do you want, carpenter?" Lucifer hissed as Yeshua approached.

"I want you to know that none of this had anything to do with you. We allowed Michael, Elaine, Destiny, and all of the beings in creation that ever cared for you to try everything they could to try and save you. Time and time, they tried reasoning, pleading, and everything they could imagine to soften your heart and lead you back to your created space. We allowed that so that when they look back on their lives, they will hold no regrets. They will know that it was your choice that led to your destruction." Yeshua's calm voice was tinged with sadness.

"You think You are so perfect, Son of Man! I have led them astray! I will continue to lead them away from You! I will have an army that far surpasses Your own!" Lucifer roared.

"You were the signet of perfection, full of wisdom and perfect in beauty. You were in Eden, the garden of God; Every precious stone was your covering."

"Be quiet!" she yelled.

"You who know the scriptures so well should remember Ezekiel 28. 'On the day that you were created they were prepared. You were an anointed guardian cherub. I placed you; you were on the holy mountain of God; in the midst of the stones of fire you walked.'"

"You did nothing!" Snarls and grunts were being thrown from the devil.

"You were blameless in your ways from the day you were created, till unrighteousness was found in you. In the abundance of your trade you were filled with violence in your midst, and you sinned."

"Stop talking! Now!"

"So I cast you as a profane thing from the mountain of God, and I destroyed you, O guardian cherub, from the midst of the stones of fire."

"No more!"

"Your heart was proud because of your beauty; you corrupted your wisdom for the sake of your splendor. I cast you to the ground; I exposed you before kings, to feast their eyes on you. By the multitude of your iniquities, in the unrighteousness of your trade, you profaned your sanctuaries; so I brought fire out from your midst; it consumed you, and I turned you to ashes on the earth in the sight of all who saw you. All who know you among the peoples are appalled at you; you have come to a dreadful end and shall be no more forever."

"You haven't won anything yet!"

"Silence. I had given you everything that you could have possibly wanted and more, but for you, it was never enough. You loved yourself so much that you became your own idol. You worshiped yourself until you needed others to worship you as well. You threw away your true identity for something that was never meant to be."

Lucifer was breathing so hard it looked as if her ribs might crack. She was trying to defy the command given to her by Yeshua but was completely unable. The hatred for Him was shown from the expression on her contorted face.

Sure Fire | Michaeli Tom

"I never wanted this for you. I never wanted this for any of you. I wanted you to choose me, but I must honor your decisions." Pity and sorrow filled His tone and marred His face with a look of heartbreak.

"The time is almost up. I know you can feel it as well as I can." He was searching her face for something Elaine wasn't sure.

"All choices have been made then. I will see you at the final appointed time."

As soon as He was finished speaking, Lucifer vanished from her place before Him. Elaine watched as He turned to face her, and His sorrowful face turned into one of love and peace. She had no clue what the gravity of her efforts actually was until she heard Him tell Lucifer why He had allowed it. He was allowing them to try every route available to them in order to free themselves from any guilt they may have once it is all said and done.

He allowed her to choose her fate, even after He showed her everything He had done for her. He honored her choice to remain outside of His presence. All He wanted was an honest relationship with her, just as He desires with the mortals. Yet, He allows each being to choose for themselves without Him forcing them to pick Him. Elaine was overwhelmed and staring at Yeshua as He stood before them.

"Where did she go?" Elaine asked in a confused voice.

"Back to earth. Her time is short, and she recognizes it very well. She will do all she can to disrupt the plans I have for the world, but I am in control."

"What do we do now?"

"Well, if you can get Michael to quit being so formal, we can finally bring you home," He said with the most genuine smile she had ever seen.

Michael immediately stood up at attention as if he were awaiting orders. Elaine couldn't help but giggle at his overly serious attitude. He looked so rigid and completely immovable. His posture reminded Elaine of all the Renaissance statues.

"Is he always like this?" Elaine jested.

"He is the best soldier We ever made. He will adjust after a little while. Being in my presence after such a long time outside of it has profound effects on all."

"Why am I not acting differently?" Elaine said, concerned as to why she wasn't affected the same as Michael.

"You are. You ran to Me as soon as you realized who I was. You have stood your ground against Lucifer. You have even made a joke with someone that is not Michael. You haven't been this free in decades. Close to Me is where you can truly be yourself." The warmth of His voice melted Elaine's heart.

Tears were beginning to well up in her eyes as she looked at her salvation standing before her. Once more, she ran to Him and hugged Him as if her life depended on it. She was so incredibly happy that she was finally able to put all of the chaos and turmoil behind her. Now, she just got to be in the presence of the One who made her who she is.

After a moment, Yeshua said, "Are you ready to go home?"

Elaine was elated once more to have an actual home to go to. She didn't even know what she expected her home to be, where it would be, or if she would be sharing it with anyone; would she have a pet?

Yeshua started laughing, and it was the purest sound Elaine had ever heard. "Come. So much has changed while you two were away. I am sure there are people that you would like to be reunited with, but first, let us go before the Father. He has been expecting us."

Elaine grabbed Michael's hand and looked toward the large open archway before her. She had survived all the trials and tribulations that had been thrown at her, and she was finally on the threshold of being in the place where she belonged. The place that her soul longed to be. The place in which she could be in the presence of the One who pieced together each aspect of who she should be.

Everything that she had gone through was for a reason. Her life on earth was to be lived for the benefit of those around her. Point them back in the way they are to go. Her time with Jeremiah was so that he could free himself from Lucifer's hold. The amount of effort spent on Lucifer was for all the ones who once loved her so that they could be free from wondering what would have happened if someone tried to bring her back. She had completed all the tasks that the Creator had set for her to go after. Now, her mortal life was completed. It was time for her to take on her new celestial role.

"I am ready," Elaine said with a smile on her face and endless possibilities in her heart.

"Then follow Me," said Yeshua as they embarked on her biggest adventure yet.

author's note

I would like to take a moment to tell you all that I am very thankful to everyone who reads this book. Writing this book literally saved my life. I was raised in church and went to a private Christian school throughout my childhood, and like many Christians, I suffered through a lot of church hurt. I quit going to church and pushed away from anyone and anything that had strong Christian values for quite a long time.

I was never angry with God, nor did I doubt His existence, but I did completely stop reading my Bible. That is until my sister-in-law, Maghan, asked me to start having a Bible study with her in her home. I was very reluctant because I wondered what could possibly be in the Bible that I hadn't already heard preached on over five times. The true reason I went was so that I could spend more time with her.

That is the thing with God, though; He will use even the smallest yes and turn it into a miracle. He began speaking to us through His Word every week that we held a Bible study. He turned my reluctance into an all-consuming hunger for the Word. The more I read, the more passages seemed as if He were telling me to put them into a book.

The specific idea for this book was from a dream that He had sent me of this large angel trying to navigate the wilderness with a sassy, headstrong, independent woman. The more I typed, the more words flowed onto the page. Every time I hit a wall, I would find something else that would reignite the flow of words.

I wanted everything that I wrote in this book to serve as a giant arrow back to Christ. I wanted to offer insight and different views that may not have been shared before. Most of all, I wanted to share the love God has for each and every one of us. Things may not be how you had envisioned them to be, but trust that He has a plan that far surpasses our understanding. His plan is full of goodness and love that knows no bounds. All we have to do is accept his gift of salvation, for there is no way for us to earn our way into heaven.

Jesus has died, been buried, and rose from the grave so that we would no longer be bound for death. He will never turn His back on you. He will never forsake you. He will never forget you.

How do I know? Because He has never given up on me. Even when I ran from Him, He welcomed me back with open arms, for He is good, kind, loving, and the only One worthy of praise. I pray that this book blesses you and renews your dependence upon your only salvation.

With all love,

michaeli tom

scripture glossary

This book was one of the main sources of reigniting my faith and hunger to know our Creator on a deeper level. I spent time praying that the Lord would open my eyes to things that I had not seen before, the outlook that He had on the scriptures, as well as opening my eyes to any scripture that I had wrong understandings on. Asking Him to make each story real and applicable to my life has changed the way that I read the Bible. He has been able to make something I thought I knew into something filled with wonder and so much love. I hope that this glossary can serve as a place for you to get started on your journey to a more understanding relationship with Christ. I have made this glossary into a roadmap for you to study through the Bible with me.

- The story of creation is found in Genesis 1.

- "Let us make man in our image" (Genesis 1:26).

- The story of God forming man out of the dust of the ground is found in Genesis 2:7.

- The story of the fall of man is in Genesis 3.

- The story of Cain is in Genesis 4:1–16.

- "Before I formed you in the womb I knew you" (Jeremiah 1:5).

- Ezekiel 28:13–19 is quoted in the last chapter of the book. This is the Lord speaking through Ezekiel to Lucifer. This is important because it shows us who Lucifer was supposed to be, the choices he made to turn from God, and the pride he has that keeps him rooted in evil.

- The story of the woman at the well can be found in John 4:4–42. I think that this woman is often misunderstood or misrepresented. It can sometimes be easy to overlook her, but Jesus went out of His way just to be able to speak to her. He knew who she was and what her purpose was as only He can.

- The story of Michael standing against Lucifer for Moses' body is in Jude 9. This is an important story to know because even the Archangel Michael didn't attempt to judge Lucifer. When he was opposed, he only replied, "The Lord rebuke you." He did not try and challenge him on his own authority, but gave the issue to God so that it would be handled according to His will.

- The story of Michael casting the angels out of heaven can be found in Revelation 12:7–12.

Printed in the USA
CPSIA information can be obtained
at www.ICGtesting.com
CBHW081606280224
4776CB00005B/95